Winner of the

6th International

Three-Day Novel

Writing Contest . . .

"Summertime is for suckers. They say it must be marvelous, being able to come down any time you want. I tell them, once or twice a week you think you're in heaven. The rest of the time you could slit your throat.

"They don't believe me."

This Guest of Summer

Jeff Doran

PULP PRESS BOOK PUBLISHERS
1984

THIS GUEST OF SUMMER
COPYRIGHT © 1984 JEFF DORAN

ISBN 0-88978-151-6

PUBLISHED BY PULP PRESS BOOK PUBLISHERS
986 Homer Street, No. 202
Vancouver, B.C. Canada v6b 2w7
A division of Arsenal Pulp Press Book Publishers Ltd.

TYPESETTING: Baseline Type & Graphics Cooperative
PRINTING: First Folio Printing Company Ltd.

PRINTED AND BOUND IN CANADA

This guest of summer,
The temple-haunting martlet, does approve
By his lov'd mansionry that the heaven's breath
Smells wooingly here.

— BANQUO, in *Macbeth*

I

THE AUCTION AT THE OLD FORREST HOME SPILLED ITS CONTENTS
out onto the lawn, as if it were an animal on the roadside,
slowly bleeding. The auctioneer was the man who called bingo
at the volunteer fire department garden parties. He kept the
crowd near the front door by promising bigger things to come.
All that was seen of Mr. Forrest was a hand which kept passing
items out through the mud porch door; they were not very big
items. A tin enamel breadbox with a faded decal of a wild rose.
A plastic parrot on a perch, to hang in a window. A whisk
broom for the stove top, worn and blackened like the epaulet of
a uniform in a museum.

When Mr. Forrest handed out a kitchen chair with the legs
sawed off, the crowd laughed, and the auctioneer took the
chance to keep them on his side.

'This is for when you're falling down drunk! So you won't have to fall so far!'

Mr. Forrest's mother had been dropsical in her last years, and her legs had swollen like sausages, linked at the knee and ankle. The only way she had been able to sit was with her legs straight, so she ate sitting on the floor like a Japanese, or like a dog, until she died. Mr. Forrest did not laugh at the auctioneer's joke. Inside the house, alone, handing his belongings out into the sun and the money on the front lawn, he was crying.

It had been his arrangement to select the order of items to be sold, and he had already told the auctioneer the set prices for certain items, like Grammy's rocker, the scimitars of wood worn flat on the oilcloth floor as if in battle. He wanted the bidding to start at twenty-five dollars for that. The mounted deer head, eight-point. His father had shot it on their own land, out of season, and he had scattered the offal in the woods for the ravens. He had butchered the carcass in the carriage shed by lantern light with the big doors closed, and had kept the head under sawdust and ice until he could safely take it to the taxidermist, a man who was also janitor at the consolidated school and couldn't keep his mouth shut. The sutured lips of the deer and the staring glass-ball eyes seemed straining to speak the misdeed. Mr. Forrest wanted fifty dollars for the head. It was worth more than the rocker because it had belonged to a man.

The crowd was drifting away from the front door, impatient with the boxes of kitchen cutlery and bags of old milk bottles. The men went to look at the machinery in the barn — the horse-drawn mower and rake, the sleigh with cowlicks of straw coming out of the black upholstery, the side-mould plow, the spring-tooth harrow, and the hay tedder. The hay tedder was agreed to be the only valuable thing in the barn, and the men were already bidding on it in their minds as they stood around it in the moted sunlight on the threshing floor. A hay tedder was hard to find these days, and with it you could put up your hay in a day, maybe a couple days earlier. Plus it was an exciting even a little comical thing to watch in action, flipping through the windrows of mown hay like a ghost army of men with pitchforks, flinging the drying grass into the air to turn it magically into hay. The men bid silently in their minds and they patted the rolls of money they had brought in the pockets of their bib overalls. They rolled cigarettes, and some of them rested with their boots possessively on the axle of the tedder. The only time you found a hay tedder nowadays was at an auction like this, when someone had died, or was about to die.

In the barn, the men waited for Mr. Forrest to get around to his business.

When his parents had died, he had already started to sell off the farm before the real estate lady came by in her station wagon. She pretended to be ignorant about practical things like farming and machines, but she knew enough about a practical thing like money. She told him to stop selling off the larger items. He had already sold the tractor and the Enterprise white enamel combination oil and wood stove. She told him he could make more with an auction, or maybe he could sell the place lock, stock and barrel to someone from the city, someone who wanted a farm complete. Not so they could do any farming. Just so they could say they had the stuff.

Mr. Forrest opted for the auction. He knew some of the things in the house were antiques, because a Jew from New York City had come through one summer offering money for old furniture. Mr. Forrest knew he had a valuable table in the parlour. He called it his Duncan Five.

There was an antique buyer tapping at the rear window, the one that faced the lake. The blind was drawn, its chalkboard green making the dining room cool, like a ferny glade. Mr. Forrest knew it was an antique buyer without looking.

'When are the antiques coming?' the man asked.

'You be patient,' said Mr. Forrest. 'I got a Duncan Five table coming.'

'Can I see it?'

'You wait out front with the rest of them.'

The rest of them were already wandering into the shade of the twin apple trees by the woodhouse, or back to their cars to sit and listen to the radio and wait for the good stuff to come out. There was rumour of a bird's eye maple dresser and a dovetail jointed cedar hope-chest. Those who knew the Forrests were remembering what they had seen in the house. They didn't know what he had already sold, though. He wasn't talking. And he was very cheerful on the telephone, a party line.

The auction had been advertised in the weekly paper, in a box with a black border, two columns wide. The dirt road to the Forrest farm was walled on both sides with vehicles, and from the kind they were you knew the kinds of people who drove them. There were the Volvos and BMW's of the people from Halifax, antique dealers, most of them. There were the pickups and stake side trucks of the men who had come planning to take home some heavy machinery. And there were the humble, sedate sedans, the Pontiac Acadians and the Valiants and Fairlanes in dull solid colours—dead fish green and inner tube red—of the local people who had come for the entertainment, not to buy anything really, unless it was as a joke, a funny hat or a 'mystery box' that rattled and turned out to contain old insulators from an electric fence. These people had brought their children. They had dressed for the occasion as if for church, the old women sitting in front with their hats pinned to grey twisted buns. The children were too hot to sit in the car; they ran on the lawn and looked for things to throw at each other. They did not know Mr. Forrest. They did not share with their parents and grandparents the unspoken solemnity of the moment when a man's worldly possessions get turned into cold cash. Mr. Forrest was going to move into a housekeeping apartment in town. He was going to divide up his money for as many years as he figured he would live yet, and he was going to try and live off that and if he didn't manage, well, let the government worry about that.

The children found the peonies in the front garden, and they pulled them up and made them into spears they could throw at each other. No one stopped them. The crowd around the front door had dwindled enough so the children were easily seen, tugging up the long stalks and shooting them through the air like feathered rockets. Some still had the roots in a clump and these they swung like clubs, batting each other with the dirt. Those who didn't know the children wondered for a moment if they should say something to them but it was done, after all; the flowers were killed. And it was an auction, after all, and the farm was going to a buyer from the city probably, maybe from as far away as Toronto, and he would never know if there had been flowers here.

The parents of the children didn't see. On days like this when they took their children somewhere, to the garden party or the yearly exhibition, they didn't want to see the children until it was time to come back to the car. Then from the dirt and sticky stuff on their hands, they saw evidence of how they had spent their day, but they didn't want to hear about it. That was the silent agreement between children and parents in the little community.

More antique dealers had taken to trying to peek through the window shades. They circled the house as if Mr. Forrest were a renegade holed up in there.

'When are the antiques coming out?'

'Hold your water!' came the voice from inside, a voice in motion, as Mr. Forrest shuttled from room to room coordinating things to hand out, as he heard the auctioneer's tireless voice intoning figures, joking about even the most sacred articles, reminding them of the sales tax. Mr. Forrest was not crying anymore. He had done with that. He was thinking about his new apartment in town, and he was thinking about what a bind it would put the government in if he ran out of money before he died.

It was hot in the house but he kept all the windows closed so no one could raise a shade and see in. It was like working in a hay loft, which seems cool in the dark at first, then becomes an airless cell, like a black exhaust pipe. Mr. Forrest wanted to keep the people on the lawn waiting as long as he could, waiting in the sun with the black flies stirred into a frenzy by all the feet in the grass. He parcelled things out in stingier and stingier bundles, once handing out a single necktie with the knot preserved in it. His father had had the son of the post master tie it for him. The son was going to Dalhousie. The tie was kept on the doorknob in the bedroom, and on Sundays old Mr. Forrest noosed it around his neck, as if donning an ox yoke for service.

The auctioneer gasped a few exasperated words back into the mud porch. Then he told the crowd he was taking a break to wet his whistle. The crowd before him consisted of eight people who had fallen under the mesmeric spell of his voice. When he went inside the house, they were released like crumbs shaken from a tablecloth.

'You're losing them,' the auctioneer said, after he had finished a glass of well water from the tap. In the cellar the piston pump banged with the sound of a boat pulling away from a dock. 'I'm not losing them. You are. I got a barrel full of junk on the porch there that'll never get sold. You better start collecting stuff in bigger bunches or get to the good stuff before they give up on you or the only ones left'll be the ones who just came for the fun, and they don't have any money.'

'I know what I'm doing,' Mr. Forrest said. 'I know I got antiques in here. If I let those go, no one'll stay for the rest of it.'

'You should have sold the contents with it. Easier that way.'

'I know what I'm doing,' Mr. Forrest said, more softly, handling the next item to go out through the door, a plastic backscratcher that looked like ivory, a hand with long fingers and Chinese fingernails.

'Didn't the party who bought the place want what was in it?' The auctioneer didn't know anymore about the deal than anyone else. He had heard from someone who heard on the party line that they were from Montreal. On the phone, Mr. Forrest talked about his 'friend.' His friend was his lawyer, who drew up the papers.

'Just the bed and the table and some chairs,' Mr. Forrest said.

'Small family?'

Mr. Forrest was staring at the fake mantle on the wall, thinking how to get rid of the glass animals his mother had collected from the boxes of tea.

'No family.'

'Young people, are they?'

Mr. Forrest looked up suddenly. He took the empty water glass and rinsed it out in the sink and set it upside down to dry so he could sell it later.

'I don't know and I don't care,' he said. 'Their money's good. That's all I know.'

'You haven't met them?'

'I don't have to meet them to cash my cheque.'

'They didn't come down...'

'I don't know and I don't care! That ain't my business, selling the house. My business is moving into town and being well rid of this place.'

He handed the auctioneer the backscratcher.

'No regrets about leaving?'

Mr. Forrest spoke past the auctioneer's face, as if he were blowing something off his cheek. 'Mister man, I'll tell you something. For all I care, this plot of land and the house and barn and outbuildings and stock fence can cave in and go to hell for all I care. And so too for the whole damn county, and everybody in it for all I care. That's how I feel about it, and that's how I feel about them, too. And I don't care if they know it.'

'Well, I'll tell you,' said the auctioneer, going out onto the mud porch with the plastic backscratcher in his hand, 'I think they're starting to get that idea.'

He had stood on his wooden chair in the doorway, looking out across the lawn and the dirt driveway with the wall of silent cars with sunglazed windshields hiding the faces inside. He was thinking about how he was going to gather them back again with just a fake Chinese backscratcher and he actually looked over the garden before he saw what they had done. It was easy to miss what they had done, because if you hadn't known there had been a flower garden there before, you wouldn't have missed it now that it was gone.

The dark hollow of earth was trodden with boot heels and furrowed with fingers. There was no colour of leaf or blossom left in it. Around it, odd remnants were withering in the sun but most had been carried away or thrown into the tall grass along the driveway. There was no one on the lawn. It was quiet enough that the auctioneer could hear the electric whine of a hatch of gnats which clung together in front of his face, as if locked inside an invisible chimney.

He felt a moment of fear, as if the people were just behind him, ready to pull the supports from the house itself. It was the awful quiet that did it. Not even a baby crying. And the glaring windshields of the vehicles that waited. Then he heard the laughter from the back yard, distant, as if it were coming from the far side of the lake. It was a busy, engaging sound, like the sound from a contest at a field day, the sound of people being urged on by others. It was coming from the vegetable garden. From his position on top of the chair, the auctioneer could see over the low woodhouse roof well enough to see the stalks of corn flying into the air, sprinkling dirt from their roots like sprays of fireworks, and cabbage heads tossed like footballs falling to unknown arms, and broccoli thrown like hats in celebration, and with each uprooting there was the approval of the crowd.

The auctioneer did not want to go behind the house to watch. It was not his job to leave the chair. He had been hired to empty the house, and he would stay in the doorway until his audience came back. He knew these people. He knew they would come back after they had entertained themselves. But he had not thought they would do this while the former owner was still on the premises. He had thought they would wait until he was gone. Until the house was vacant. Or until the new owners moved in, showed their faces, and then left the house unattended for a weekend. It disquieted him that people would do such a thing while you were still close at hand, alive and watching. He used to think that what happened to you after you were dead didn't matter because you wouldn't know about it anyway, but now he saw these people treating Mr. Forrest as if he were dead, and he was not. He was still inside the dark house looking for something to hand out next.

The auctioneer held the long sharp fingers of the plastic hand in front of his face, and he called out to himself:

'Hey-a! Hey-a! Look what I got he-yah! Who's gonna start the biddin'? Hey-a! Hey-a! The good stuff is comin' now!'

II

IT WAS NIGHT WHEN JACK MILFORD DROVE HIS WIFE THERESE AT last up the narrow driveway to the old Forrest home. The headlights of the little blue Renault flared briefly across the downstairs windows of the house as the car crested a little rise near the front lawn, making the house look occupied. Jack felt a moment of panic as he thought that something had gone wrong, that all the phone calls and the documents sent by mail, and all the trust he had put in the realtor and the bank and Canada Post had failed him. But no one was at home. The house was theirs and theirs alone.

Thérèse was asleep against the door. She had slept all the way from Halifax, two hours, after they had got lost in the city, being swept into it by the Trans-Canada, taking the wrong exit which led them inexorably toward bridges and city streets. She had been sleeping most of the way since they had entered New Brunswick. The Trans-Canada frightened her with its path through woodland, and she was not reassured by the exit signs with promises of coffee cups and knives and forks. Until now she had not been east of Trois-Rivières. When they had crossed the first new border, she had said, 'Now we'll stop for an ice cream to celebrate,' and they had looked and looked for an ice cream stand, a restaurant, a canteen, a grocery, and then they had found themselves close to the town where they had a reservation at the Wandlyn. By the time they had checked in, the dining room was closed so they had bought chocolate bars and cans of pop from the vending machine in the hallway. They had sat on the pebbled bedspread, watching themselves in the big mirror over the bureau, and Thérèse had forlornly twirled the dial of the colour TV. It got two channels, and one of them, the CBC, was a test pattern before long.

To be fair, Jack had not asked Thérèse to help with the driving. She did not want the house, she did not want to go to Nova Scotia this summer, she did not agree that thirty-five hundred was a steal for a piece of lake-frontage even if the house and buildings had to be bulldozed, she did not see a future for herself summering away from Montreal, she did not have fond memories of grandparents' farm houses when she was a child, so Jack did not ask her to drive.

He was tired, and he lay back on the bed still clothed and fell asleep listening to Thérèse click the stations of static. When he awoke in the night, his feet tingling from where he was dangling his legs over the edge, Thérèse was a wrinkle in the other double bed and he had to pat the covers to find her between the pillows. He felt the muscle of the shoulder, almost indistinguishable from bone. It fitted his palm like a billiard ball.

'You won't like sleeping with a dancer,' someone had told him, even before he and Thérèse had started sleeping together. 'Their bodies are like varnished wood.'

Now that he thought about it, the person who had told him was a dancer himself, and he was talking about sleeping with men, but he wasn't that far off. In the three years they had lived together, one year married, Jack had grown accustomed to feeling the body of his wife in his arms like some multi-handled wooden tool, perfectly hinged and balanced, strong and unyielding. And even in the softest parts of her he had found, there had been always a ring of muscle, a ridge of taut skin tensed as if for a leap. Now as he ran his hand over her short-cropped hair, he thought of an acorn cap. Thérèse to him was like the pixie on the badges of Brownies who came to the door of their apartment on Rue Oisille selling cookies. Even when she weighed less than a hundred pounds, when she was in top shape and working steady, she had the atomized power of an ensign, a magical insignia, and at the same time he knew she could slip through keyholes and between his fingers. Taking her to Nova Scotia with him to look at their farm was one way of holding her for a little while. He drove with her beside him, and she was trapped in the car by its high speed and by the desolation of the roadway. When he got her to the farm, she would not be able to spring high enough or stride far enough to get away from him.

It was his two-week vacation from the company, his own company. He had given himself the vacation, leaving his partner to finalize the details with the Ottawa school board for the soft-ware programme they were selling them. Thérèse had a week before her company started their Western tour. Then he would not see her again until the fall. She had said she would stay home with him if he wanted for a few days; maybe they could take a drive north, find a cabin for overnight. But he knew wherever they were she would be poised, flexed, her toes tapping time to inner music.

'Look, if you hate it, you can fly back the next day,' he had promised her.

'Do they have an airport in Nova Scotia?' she had said.

She had her ticket in her suitcase: Halifax to Montreal to Calgary. He knew she thought it was stupid to be driving all this way just so she could see his farm, and then to turn around and fly back, laying over an hour in Montreal which didn't even give her time to stop by the apartment and have a decent shower.

He resisted the temptation to speak to her when she was asleep. It was too lonely hearing only his voice, but he said her name to see if she would wake up.

'Tres?'

Her hair bristled slighly under his touch. It was freshly cut and not long enough to lie flat.

'Tres?'

He sat beside her on the bed, laying one leg along the curve of her body. She had pulled the sheet and the blanket and the bedspread as well tight around her shoulders. He lay carefully beside her, on top of the covers, still in his clothes, and flipped off his shoes over the end of the bed and put his head on his arm, for she had left him no pillow.

In the morning she would say, 'Why didn't you sleep in your own bed?'

HE WOKE HIS WIFE WITH HER NAME AND A HAND ON THE ACORN cap of hair.

'Tres?'

She snapped awake, one arm slapped against the door of the Renault.

'Huh?'

She made the little chipmunk sounds with her mouth she always made when waking up suddenly, smacking and sucking noises that came before speech.

'Where are we?'

'We're here.'

'Where?'

'Here. The farm.'

She leaned her temple against the black glass and let her eyes roll past the windshield and out the window on Jack's side.

'Where?'

Jack was out of the car. In a few steps he had disappeared into the dark, and Thérèse could see only her reflection in the glass from the overhead light. His voice came to her.

'Come on out. It's beautiful.'

She did not know what it was that was supposed to be beautiful. There was a feeling that Jack had parked under a highway overpass, that something large was looming over them. Cautiously she got out of the car and stood beside it, touching its cool metal.

What was looming over them was a starless patch of sky which was the shoulder of the house. And overhead was the flawed symmetry of the night sky, a confusion of stars in clusters and belts that suggested no formation. She had been to a planetarium once where the ant-like projector had thrown a whorl of pinpoints over her that had made her the centre of everything, then the universe had rotated with her as the spindle, and it had given her the feeling of falling and she had clutched the arms of her seat. But there was no motion to this sky this night. She rocked her head to make the stars move, and they did, but only like the waving of a paint brush of speckles.

'Isn't it stupendous!' Jack said, his voice rebounding from

what must have been the wall of the house. 'Money can't buy this.'

'Your money did.'

Certain things were clear. It was his money. It was his farm. It was supposed to be their farm but it was his farm, and even he knew it, although he insisted on saying otherwise. Her money didn't buy anything. It kept her training, studying, traveling, and it had gotten her the apartment in the first place, the one that had become theirs, but it didn't buy anything really, not even clothes. Most of the grant money the company got went to pay the choreographers. It was understood that the dancers either lived off their families, lived poor, or they married rich. Jack wasn't rich, but he could be. He wanted to be. He didn't say as much but it was clear. It was a simple desire. He kept a brochure of the Mercedes Benz with his trade magazines, and on the highway he pointed out the cars to Thérèse like a little boy naming them.

'Look!' he would say. 'How old do you think that guy is?'

Jack was twenty-eight. He told Thérèse that it was all right if he worked eighteen hours a day getting the company going because he was young, he could take it.

'Then I can retire when I'm forty-five.'

'You could retire when you're forty-five if you were in the army," she said. 'And you wouldn't be hurting your body in the process, not enough sleep, the wrong kind of food, drinking to stay awake, drinking to go to sleep. . . .'

'I'm not saying I'll be in computers all my life,' he said. 'This real estate thing might be the place to be. These old farms in the Maritimes are being snapped up right now. Ontario has already caught on, prices are going crazy already, for stuff with no electricity, rotten foundations, who knows what kind of chemical dump in the backyard. But in Nova Scotia it's a buyer's market. The people are moving off the farms. They want bungalows on the roadside. They want homes you get in two halves on flatbed trucks. Mobile homes. Homes with picture windows and dining-room chandeliers from Simpson's. The last thing they want in the world is the old family home to fix up. Let somebody else take off the old plaster and re-do the floors and put on the roof. It's getting done, too. There are places in the backwoods of Nova Scotia that you wouldn't believe. I hear about it from people who get invited there for a weekend. They fly into Halifax on company jets then a company limousine takes them to this country retreat, and there are indoor pools and solar heating cells and conservatory greenhouses and spiral staircases and fieldstone fireplaces. And the whole thing is protected with a chain-link fence and guard dogs. And do you know where the big money is coming from? West Germany. The West Germans are getting ready for the big move-out. When the country goes Communist, they want to have a place ready to run to. Guess where they're going to go? You think I'm going to find myself living on some homestead eating bean sprouts, some back-to-the-lander out of the 60s, come ten or fifteen years? No sir. I can take that measly investment and turn it into a hundred thou, maybe two hundred thou if the government falls, and I can sell it just the way it is. The West Germans will hire local labour to do the work, and they'll fence themselves right off the land they used to walk across. It's happening right now, Tres. And I'm on top of it.'

A light blinded her. It came from under a shade like a dish pan on the end of a gooseneck pipe, high on the corner of the house. Jack stepped into the spotlight holding a padlock and a key.

'God, I love owning things!' he said, smiling openly.

THEY SLEPT IN THE BED THAT HAD BEEN LEFT THEM, AS PER THEIR agreement with the seller. There was linen, pillows and pillow cases, and a quilt on the brown painted tubular steel frame in the empty room in which an oval table with legs as thick as young tree trunks and three chairs painted black like old car oil had been left behind. There was no trace of a man, or a family, having lived here. Even the bedclothes smelled only of flannel shut in upon itself, the smell of a stuffed toy that has ripped open.

Jack wanted to make love. Tres knew he would, and she was curious about the sound the bed would make anyway. It amused her. She sat on his lap on the side of the bed facing the open window with the rusted screen. She was leaning forward, her hands on the windowsill, and Jack had his legs over the edge of the mattress. At first he lay back flat, lazily, his arms out, while she bounced and giggled with little chirping noises, but then as she grasped the flaked wood of the sill, pulling herself tighter together he felt her muscles and sinews secure him inside her and he sat forward and grasped her around the waist, a waist so thin that he could cross his arms and grip her hipbones, and they bounced together, the bedsprings jingling and one squawking sound of strain from the metal frame every third or fourth time when he lifted against her, lifting her buttocks with his right off the mattress as he pressed with his arms beside and behind him until finally they were standing and he moved his hands up to her breasts which were drawn tight over the muscles in two rasping nipples, rough as chapped skin, and the bed was silent.

'No!' Thérèse gasped with air pumped out of her and she butted herself back against him so they landed on the bed and made it jingle again, because the jingling was making her laugh and the laughing was making her come as the laughing became a sound that made him think she was ready to come and made her think that she was going to come until she did make a sound that sounded like she was coming, a sound, part of the laughing and the ringing tambourine of the bed and the scraping of its metal parts until she didn't know if she was making the sound or if it was just happening and she didn't know if she wanted him to think she was coming or if she really was, but it was so easy to let the sound out in the hollow room in the empty house in the lightless night and she let it out until she thought the bed would break and the sound would wake the world, almost with a fierceness lifting herself off his shank and stretching with her chest arched at the window screen where mosquitoes grasped the mesh and probed into the warm body smell of the occupied room, then doubling herself to drive herself back upon him, and when she was bent like that something inside of her gripped him like a fist, a selfish grasp and she thought she could feel every rib, every fold and ridge and swollen vessel of his member and she heard him murmur a sound that began Holy something and now she was fucking him, she was making him come, he was the one who was coming for the first real time and she drove in and out of him and he gave himself up and lost his link with her arms and her chest and he flung himself back upon the mattress where she worked on him facing away into the limitless night outside the insect humming screen where she was staring eyes wide into what she didn't know, what wouldn't be revealed even in the morning, and her sound was mingled with his now, it was laughter, triumphant and joyous, laughter at being granted what was owed, what the human race had been dealt from the beginning, laughter close to tears, that was the whole organism shuddering at once into being, the laugh, the cry, the bawling suck of air of coming naked into the night.

THE MOSQUITOES FOUND THEIR WAY IN BEFORE DAWN. THE small frame of the woman hid itself from their sound under the blankets, pressed against the body of the man, huge, like the edge of a continent in the dark. She pulled herself against his chest, her nose pressed into the hairs which began at the soft hollow of his throat, and she hid herself by him as if pulling herself into sleep, but she was not sleeping. She was fitting her legs, shins as slender as the man's wrist, thighs muscled like stretched elastic, between his legs, hot and damp where they were pressed together as he lay on his side, and she was forcing his legs apart, doing something she had never done, not in all the nights they had slept together. She was waking him up to make love again.

III

'YOU'RE PRETTY SEXY WHEN YOU'RE GETTING YOUR OWN WAY,' she said when at last he came downstairs. She had had time to boil water for coffee with the little electric coil she traveled with, and she was drinking it, instant and strong and black, as she waited for him. There were no cups on the shelves of the cupboards, and she had had to use the cup from the thermos jug. She offered it to him as he sat down across the black table from her, but he made her put the cup down and he took her hands instead.

'I feel so...right!' he said, shaking his head at the ineffectiveness of the words.

'I think you are right,' she said softly. 'Whatever you are doing, don't stop it. I like it.'

'I don't know,' he said, distractedly taking the cup up and drinking from it, not knowing where he was, or whose coffee he was drinking, just that it was morning and it was coffee and he had awakened to something. 'But I've never felt this way before. It's like...' He put the cup down and she could see his hand was shaking, and she covered it with hers. 'Like I really am right this time. No doubt. Just a feeling. You can't substantiate it. You can't say "Here are the odds, my chances are such and such." You just have a feeling that you're doing the right thing. Do you know?'

For the first time that morning he looked into her eyes. She saw the flicker of recognition, and she saw him almost lose the moment as sensations of hunger and weariness and wanting to take a shower and shave and drive to the nearest donut place for a glazed cruller threatened to take over, and she tried to help him keep that feeling.

'I know the feeling,' she said. 'It's what I always told you I felt when I knew I was ready to dance. Before an audition, or even minutes before I go onstage, if I get that feeling, I know it's going to be right. If I don't get that feeling, it's okay too. It's life. They don't know the difference out there anyway. But when you have that feeling, it's more than life, isn't it?'

'Yes!' He took her hands again. 'It's being in the right place at the right time of everything.'

'Being at the centre of the stars,' she said.

'Jesus! Do you think it's the water or something? Are we freaking out on some kind of mold?'

'Jack,' she said, bringing his hands around her hands to her lips and kissing with light dry touches all around his encircling thumb and forefinger so that she felt the coil of hairs on the backs of his knuckles. 'You are twenty-eight years old. A lot of other men turn twenty-eight and there is nothing ahead of them except being twenty-nine and then thirty and then thirty-five, and they will not be rich men when they are thirty-five, or forty-five, but I think you have discovered this year that you are not going to be one of those men. You are going to be a special man.'

'I think I'm bloody well going to be a rich man,' he said with a little laugh. 'God, what a place to discover it!'

'Well,' she said, 'it is your mountain top. You cannot choose where enlightenment will hit you.'

He brought her closer to him, drawing her to him with her hands still in his, and he rose and leaned across the wide black table to kiss the space between her eyebrows.

'I'm glad you came,' he said. 'You're good luck.'

She could hear him through the little screened window in the peak of the roof, rattling boards in the attic. He had gone looking for a cooking pot, a pan, anything. She stood outside, squinting against the sun over the eaves. She had gone out to see what was in the garden. She had found first the two apple trees, but the apples were still yellow, and they looked dwarfed, like soft chestnuts.

'The old bugger cleaned the place out!' Jack called to her. There was a muffled sound of skull on rafter and Jack cursed.

'Well, you told him you didn't want any of the, what do you call it, cattle?'

'Chattel. It comes from the same word.' She heard him moving across the boards to the window, and then she saw his face pressed against the dark screen, as if he were trapped inside a blackened TV screen, and he spoke to her as if he were giving an extension course in real estate to people smoking their first cigarette of the day with their first cup of coffee. 'They come from the same word, actually. They both come from *capital*. But now, I didn't want any of his cattle or his chattel but I wouldn't mind a single goddamn stew pot to boil a Christly egg in!'

'I told you we could drive somewhere. I don't mind. I'm not that hungry.' She chewed idly on an unripe apple, and then looking down it was like chewing her own pale knuckle, and she tossed it away with a shudder.

'No, I told you I brought groceries. You don't think I'd move us in here without that much, do you. The goddamn bugger left us without so much as a pot to pee in!'

'Where's the nearest town? I'll drive over and buy you a pot if you want one.'

'The nearest town is. . .' His voice was moving away from the window and she lost what he said in the sound of his stumbling in the dark. It was a matter of pride now, she knew, and he wouldn't be argued out of it. Not the way he was feeling now. She looked down the dirt drive that sank into a bed of green that was treetops, and rose beyond them in a curl of brown snake caught in the sun.

'How about a neighbour, then? I'll borrow something.'

She heard him mutter to himself something that began 'Just a Christly. . .' his voice strangely loud and clear, projected by the angle of the roof. He sounded preoccupied.

'Have you found something?'

'There's something. . .' Again he seemed to be speaking to himself. She pictured him on his hands and knees in the attic, spanning the beams, splinters in his fingers, hairnets of cobweb caught behind his ears and inside his collar.

'Ow! Goddamn son of a whore!'

'What is it?' She shielded her eyes against the sun coming over the roof and tried to see into the dark window.

'Jesus! Something bit me or. . .'

'Bit you!' She ran to the side of the house under the attic window. She had felt a chill at the thought of something living in the attic, just a thickness of wallpaper over their heads last night. She didn't know what lived in attics and bit people. Bats? Rats?

He hadn't spoken and she called his name angrily. His voice came back suddenly calm, preoccupied again. This time he said wonderingly to himself 'Son of a whore,' then to her, 'I'm coming down.'

'Come down,' she said, and she felt herself stamp the ground a little. She found that she was holding her arms tightly across her chest and she was shaking. She recognized the feeling. It was from lack of food. A dancer knew this. But it was something else, too. It was Jack's voice from the attic, his voice without his face, and it was her standing on the lawn by the stunted fruit tree. Did apple trees lose their leaves in the summer? Did the leaves fall before the fruit was ripe? And it was the long, barren road engulfed by the canopy of trees only after it fell to the bottom of the hill. Without knowing, she knew that the property line ended at the bottom of the hill where the green trees began. And the vegetable garden. Did people plow in summer? What had been there that had been harvested before they had come? The ground was moiled and hacked, not a shred of crop or weed in it, and around the edges only the barest, unidentifiable foliage burnt in the sun.

Jack came out holding the wrist of his right hand. On the pink pad at the base of his thumb was a bright crimson wedge, the skin lifted as if by a can opener. He put the cut to his mouth and sucked.

'What was it?' she asked, her eyes on his.

He dropped his hand and spat into the grass. 'It was fucking barbed wire if you can believe that. Fucking barbed wire in the attic, between the studs. What the fuck was he doing, keeping cattle in his attic?'

'Let me see.' She held his hand near her face. His hand was shaking too, from the wound probably as much as from hunger. She could see where the barb had stuck in and where it had torn the flesh when he had jerked his hand away.

'Barbed wire in the wall,' he was saying, still in disbelief. 'What the hell was he doing with barbed wire in the wall? I mean, it was stuck way down there. It was in there for a purpose, in between the studs. I saw some other stuff in there, some box lids and such, toppled in between the floor boards and the wall, caught in the spider webs they're so thick up there, and I thought maybe something else had fallen in, you know, something the old bugger forgot when he cleared out. And I felt this cold piece of metal and I thought it was something like a can or a lid of something, so I stuck my hand deeper down between the studs and bang, this thing bit me. Jesus, I didn't know if it was a bat or what! I ripped my hand out and I brought the wire half with me and look what I did.'

He held the hand out again stupidly, like a bewildered child.

'Are you sure it was barbed wire, not some kind of, I don't know, reinforcing or something?'

'Look, when they built these houses, they didn't know about reinforcing rods and that sort of thing. This is plain simple fucking barbed wire. And old too. I mean, the guy has got a museum of barbed wire in the walls of his house.'

'Maybe it fell there. Years ago.'

Jack sucked his palm again. 'Yeah. You store barbed wire in the attic. Barbed wire you use to build your fucking fence to keep in your fucking cattle. That you keep in the barn. You don't keep it in the attic.'

She backed slightly away from his anger.

He flung his hand at the end of his arm like trying to shake off a biting thing. 'Jesus it hurts!'

She felt her feet shifting lightly under her, as if waiting for a cue to move. 'Well . . . ?'

He flung the hand again and made it crack. 'Well, now we sure as hell are driving into town because there is no way I am going to come home from this vacation with lockjaw.'

He was trying to reach into his right pants pocket with his left hand. She held the pocket open to help him.

'Do you want me to drive?' she said.

He didn't answer. He was standing by the door to the mud porch with his keys on the leather-tooled holder, thinking. Then he reached inside around the corner of the door and took the padlock off a nail and he stood in the open doorway weighing the padlock in one hand and the keys in the other, and abruptly he hooked the lock back on its nail and bunted the door shut with his hip.

'Fuck it,' he said to the house.

IV

JACK AND THERESE WERE STILL LOOKING FOR THEIR SECOND CUP of coffee of the day, but the doctor's surgery was already busy. Jack stopped at the house with the driveway full of cars even before he reached town. It was a modern back-split, with a paved drive that curved around back to the waiting room entrance.

'How do you know this is a doctor?' Thérèse said.

'Who else do you know would have a driveway full of customers on a Saturday morning?' Jack said.

Thérèse sat in the car while he went in. There was a new looking grey door with no window, and just the words COME IN stuck by individual adhesive parallelograms beside the doorknob, the kind of letters people put on their mailboxes, that looked slanty and racy as if eager to get a job done. She waited long enough to try the radio in the Renault, finding only one clear station that was playing a bluegrass hour, and static from Halifax, and a voice distorted by the airwaves to sound like someone speaking down the end of a long pipe, that told her, in French, that it was coming from St. John. The familiar unfamiliarity of Radio-Canada pronunciation made her feel cut apart from the East, what she had called the East before coming here. Nova Scotia was an island, wasn't it? Hadn't someone cut a channel through? She felt she was on the deck of an ocean liner pulling away from the mainland, which was Montreal and the rest of civilization. She turned off the radio and went into the waiting room. She was going to lock the car, but it was already hot in the sun, and the other cars and trucks in the driveway had their windows down. Still, she felt uneasy leaving it unlocked. There was no window on this side of the basement wall, so she couldn't watch it from inside. She decided she would ask Jack if she should go back out and lock it.

The waiting room was full. There was nowhere for her to sit except on a corner of the low table slathered with magazines and comic books and Golden Books, the covers torn off or folded back. A baby sat on the floor by the table, gumming the corner of a book about a bunny. There were several men in the molded fibreglass chairs but none of them rose for her. They were wearing sagging denim trousers with grey and blue braces pulling the waist above or below their bellies as suited their comfort. There were no young men. There were women of indeterminate age dressed in shapeless faded prints of undefined flowers. Thérèse could only guess their ages by the presence of young children clustered around some of them. The oldest women held themselves alone and upright in their chairs, rigid and patient in their private pain, although Thérèse guessed that some of the old men must be their husbands. It was air conditioned in the waiting room. No one wanted to wait out in the sun, and Thérèse could not be sure which of those waiting were the injured or the infirm, and she could not tell how long a wait Jack had ahead of him. He did not speak to her, smothered as he was by the silence of the room, broken only by the splutter of the baby on the floor and the muted squabbling of brothers tormenting sisters hushed by their mothers and the long, tired, low wail of the infant held on one woman's lap, whose glossy lips she idly caressed with the nipple of a bottle.

Thérèse started to search through the layers of magazines, but the whole pile threatened to slide off the table so she held herself still and thought about going back out to the car. Then an inner door opened and a woman came out, shuffling on bandaged ankles that swelled over the sides of her black shoes. A man lifted himself from his seat by pushing up on his knees with a sigh, and the two of them left together, and another man, this one holding a towel to the side of his face, got up and went into the surgery. Thérèse did not notice until he was passing her that the underside of the towel near his face was red with blood. She sat in his seat, near the door that had opened and was shut again. She still had not seen the doctor. And why was there no receptionist? And how did people know who was next? These things bothered her, and she looked to Jack to see if they bothered him too, and he did a trick he could do with his eyeballs. By making the skin over his forehead and around his cheekbones go taut with some facial muscle control she hadn't yet been able to detect, he could make his eyes appear to bulge. What it meant was: Holy God do you believe this!

She pulled herself tall on the chair, and by pulling in the muscles of her lower back made her spine ease itself, and slowly, as if tiptoeing over a giant map of a nation, she located the muscles and joints of her body from the toes up, contracting each and holding it for a five count and then releasing. She was at her abdomen, and starting to feel good for the first time this morning, when she noticed a woman across the room staring at her. The woman was wearing a sleeveless pullover, and the slack skin on her arms where the triceps should have been was dangling like wattles. She was not wearing a bra. Her breasts were somewhere down around her lower ribs. As soon as her eyes met the stranger's, they shot up to the ceiling, and Thérèse had an image of the stares of all the people in the room lancing out into lucite shafts; seen from above the room would look like a crystal anemone. It was not like the anonymous staring of the passengers on the Metro who could look across the aisle at their own reflections in the black glass. These glances reached for the ceiling, like searchlights, intersecting somewhere above the heads of the people. Thérèse watched the woman not watching her, and she tried to imagine her forty years old, then younger, then newly married, then she tried to imagine her as her own age. She tried to find something of youth about her, even in the eyes, the tip of the nose, the knuckle of the little finger, but nothing remained that had not been ravaged. She wondered what had happened to the woman to leave her this way. And then she tried to imagine herself being this woman, looking like this, and the only way she could do it was to imagine that the woman looked this way because of something the doctor had done to her. That was when she first heard the shouting coming from the inner office.

No one else appeared to hear it. There was the flutter of the air conditioner and the ceaseless shifting of clothing as people crossed their legs and folded and unfolded their arms, and the breathing of the old women through their mouths, and of course the small mammal sounds of the babies and the children who now had lain on their backs on the cold tile floor to feel it against their skin. But Thérèse could not understand why no one else seemed to hear the shouting. It was the doctor's voice, she knew, because it sounded admonitory. He did not sound as he were sympathetic toward the man with the bleeding face.

She could not make out what he was saying, just the tone, but she was very good at making up sentences to fit a tone of voice. That was the way she had first learned English, coming from Belgium to Canada with her mother who had not fled the war like so many others but had stayed to see how many of her family would be killed and then had come with the survivor, just her daughter, when Europe was reconstructing and the flow of emigrants was not so great. Then it had been easier, and cheaper, to come, and she had been able to get the job she wanted which was just as a clerk in a Chinese novelty store. It was close to the apartment she could afford which was close to the school she wanted her daughter to attend, the ballet school on the second floor. She could stand on the sidewalk and watch her daughter whirl to and from the big windows in her lessons. It was why she had endured the war and why she had suffered the deaths of the men. The two of them, the two women, had grown up together in Montreal, little Thérèse always feeling as old as her mother, walking beside her on the street and avoiding the eyes of the men who scanned her up and down approvingly as she matured, feeling an equal in her mother's conversations in French with the other tenants, and finding that after a while of pretending she understood English, in fact she was understanding it. It always made her feel a little sorry for the language, if it was that easy to understand.

She looked at Jack again to see if he was listening to the doctor's voice but he was looking at his hand, squeezing the cut, either to make it hurt or to make it bleed. Maybe he thought he could advance his place in line if he showed some blood.

She felt a little sorry for Jack, too, for his being English and native to such an easy language. It suggested something about him that she did not like to find herself thinking, that despite his youth and his apparent virility, and despite the promise of success which had glowed around him this morning in the stripped dining room, despite the fact that he very likely could become what she knew he wanted to be, a millionaire at thirty-five, still he was, like his language, not very difficult to understand, and probably not very smart.

This kind of thinking bothered her. It was what she did when she could not be using her body. It was what her body did to her when she did not use it enough. That was why she had wanted to do the contracting and releasing exercises. She was about to go outside and do some warm-ups on the doctor's lawn no matter what anybody said when the door to the surgery was opened by the man with the bloody towel. Now he held it in one hand by his leg, as if ashamed he had brought it in, and on the side of his face, at the corner of his eye, was a little gauze patch, held with an X of flesh-coloured tape.

The doctor looked into the waiting room for the first time, as if checking the goldfish in his pond, and Thérèse knew at a glance that he was British. She knew why the voice had communicated authority by its tone, because it had a British accent, an accent she associated with tutors and directors and examiners and officers, from the radio even in Europe to the immigration officials who had made her weigh herself twice because she weighed so little; they had suggested by their tone that she was underfed, perhaps malnourished, and would be a liability in Canada, until her mother had said witheringly, *'Elle est danseuse!'*

The doctor was a beef eater, flushed and fleshed with steak-and-kidney and warm beer black as creosote. He had wild white curls of hair upon his head, as if his stuffing were coming out, and under his chin too, and the white ticking seemed to sandwich the pouches of his face, squeezing his cheeks out and reddening them like his nose. His eyebrows, she saw, were so fair as to be almost invisible against the pink skin. He reminded her of an albino who has grown fat eating other albinos. She did not think at all of Father Christmas, although that is what he would have made any Englishman think of.

'Mister. . . ?' he inquired, looking at Jack.

'Milford,' Jack said, 'but these people are ahead of me I believe.'

'Oh,' the doctor said, tipping his head as if it were severed and rolling on a platter, 'these people are all old friends of mine and are just paying me a regular friendly visit, and I'm sure they wouldn't mind letting you go ahead of them. Please.'

He gestured by holding the door open wider.

'And. . . ?'

He was raising his hairless brows at Thérèse.

'My wife,' Jack said.

'Lady Milford,' said the doctor. 'You come in as well.'

'WELL,' SAID THE DOCTOR, HOLDING JACK'S HAND IN BOTH OF HIS, 'so you've been bitten by a barbed wire fence have you?'

He let Thérèse sit in the one chair in the examining room. Jack was sitting on the padded table with the roll of paper sheeted down for the next patient. His feet did not touch the floor. It made him look like a child.

The doctor was standing, holding the cut hand very close to his eye, inhaling through his nose. Then he kept a grasp on the hand with his left, reaching behind him to a shelf for a magnifying lens. Deftly, with the fingers of one hand, he spread the lips of the wound and looked into it. Jack did not flinch, but he was holding himself away from the man, either out of pain or to keep his body out of the light.

'Nothing in there that shouldn't be in there,' the doctor said. Peering down at the hand, chin buried in his beard on his chest, he looked hunched into a single dollop, like one of those sand-weighted toys that cannot be punched over.

'Last tetanus shot?'

'That's what I'm here for.'

'Very good. Very good, very good.' He administered the injection while addressing Thérèse. 'And what, pray tell, allowed you to permit your dear husband the oversight of sticking his unworthy hands into places best kept out of?'

She did not want to answer, as if keeping her voice a secret. The doctor already seemed to know so much about them from what Jack had told him as he was filling out the card for the medical insurance. Her voice seemed the last bit of privacy she was permitted.

The doctor was waiting, presumably for the bubbles in the vial of serum to surface.

'My husband is . . .'

She thought she detected a ripple over his pink face at the way she said *husband,* the accent on the second syllable, the missing *h,* the elision with the *y,* all the dead give-aways. She paused, watching him. *Anglais.*

'*C'est un homme vrai, n'est-ce pas?*' said the doctor.

'*Oui, c'est ça.*' Her voice surprised her, the voice of a little girl, testing, trying, reaching out. Even with Jack she did not speak French very much. He pretended to understand as she had always pretended, but she could tell with him it was just pretense, it led to nothing. It was a way to pass time until she would speak English again.

The doctor held the sleeve of Jack's shirt up for him above

the muscle after the shot, letting the alcohol evaporate, and he turned his head sideways at Thérèse in a way that shielded his look from her husband, and he said, 'I consider it an honour and a privilege to be understood. Parisian?'

'Close.'

Jack was twisting his head down, trying to look at his arm, or the doctor's face, Thérèse couldn't be sure which. She saw a bulge like a big mosquito bite on his arm slowly dissipating.

'Not Québecois, I could tell for sure. I knew from the way you said *Oui*. Say it again for me if you would be so kind.'

Softly she said it. A little girl again. Shy. Admitting a liking for something, a choice in a toy shop.

'Nothing like your Canadian French,' the doctor was saying, rolling down Jack's sleeve for him. 'Theirs is a quack, a most awful thing. Wanh! Wanh!'

He made her giggle, and she covered her mouth, something she had not done since childhood, to be silent in the line at the *barre*. Jack slid off the sheet of paper with a rustling sound of a parcel being unwrapped and he landed beside his wife.

'Neighbours? I hope?' said the doctor.

'Just down for a visit,' Jack said. 'I've bought the old Forrest place. An investment really. We're here for the week. Thérèse has to fly back. . . .'

She let his voice fade into background as she watched the change come over the doctor's face when Jack had mentioned the name of the farm. It had been the same ripple of thought, as if his mind was shaking the flesh of his head like shaking a bedsheet, that she had seen when he had first heard her voice. He caught her looking at him and tried to pass off his preoccupation as embarrassment.

'I do beg your pardon. Please call me Max.'

It was the name for a dog, Thérèse thought. At least they didn't have to call him Binkie or Twinkie or Uncle Sussie or Cousin Pip or the other kinds of things the English were always degrading themselves with.

'Max from Mayfair, which may make you think of Lord

Fairfax, Mayfair-Fairfax: Max. Please do not call me Doctor
Mayfair, I shall think I am being paged, and do not ask me
my Christian name, no Christian worth his salt could have
dubbed an innocent mortal with it. Shall I tell you what it is? It
is Eliot. Eliot Mayfair. Now do you know why I am called
Max? I assure you, it weathers considerably better in the local
garage when I wish my car to be attended to. Max, if you
please, and don't ever reveal that other name of an emigré
banker. I don't even know why I told you. I suppose those who
see it in its initial assume it to be Ernest or Edgar or Evan or
Eugene. *You*-gene they say around here. All right, you are both
my beholden prisoners. I have revealed to you my true name,
surrendered to you the powers of the wizard and his demon
consorts, and you must do my bidding. Share a light lunch
with me in, say, three-quarters of an hour. Will you do that?'

All the time he had been bandaging Jack's hand, and neither
of them noticed when he was done until he shook the hand with
just the tips of his fingers as if to test it, bent forward in a slight
bow, and then took Thérèse's hand, curling the fingers around
his, the bird-thin bones in the back of her hand showing, and
held it there as if he would kiss it but he did not. He held it until
she answered.

'*Oui.*' The softest whistle of a word.

V

HAM AND CHEESE PIE, HE CALLED IT, THOUGH IT WAS QUICHE
Lorraine. 'Spartan fare, I'm afraid,' he said, serving the wedges
onto their saucers with the side of a table knife. 'Best I can do.
Maid's night out, you know.'

Thérèse knew it was an idiomatic joke, like 'busman's holiday.' It meant he was a bachelor.

And home-made beer, tawny and tasting of fresh-cut hops sparkling chaff in the sun above the reapers' blades while swallows darted ahead of them like the thoughts of wise children.

'Sorry,' he said, 'it's from a mix. I got it in the local Red and White. I was fed up with trying to make the hours of the Liquor Commission, and I decided if my alternative was to go to someone they called a bootlegger, I would be my own bloody bootlegger. Do you know what a bootlegger is around here? Not a man who makes the stuff in his bathtub. It's a man with a driver's license and a big trunk, and he takes the money of those who can't drive for one reason or another, or, like me, find the hours inconvenient, and he buys it for them strictly legal, right off the shelf, and transports it home for them, and for that he collects his tariff. Not for me. I manufacture it in my own casks right here in the surgery, and I siphon it myself and bottle it myself. I even have my own little capping machine I purchased at the local Farmers' Cooperative.'

He took a swallow from the glass mug.

'Horrid stuff, isn't it,' he said, making a face.

I know what he looks like, Thérèse thought. He looks like one of those upside down faces you can look at either way in the funny papers. The beer was syrupy and smelled of turf and polystyrene, but it was potent, and it was the first she had drunk of anything since the morning's coffee. Jack was on his second mug.

They had gone looking for a delicatessen or a Mini-Mart in their forty-five minutes, to buy something to contribute toward brunch, and had found nothing except an Irving station with a man down a concrete pit under a Dodge Fargo, and a house that sold grotesque mammoth plywood butterflies for the exterior walls of your house, and wretched little Tweedle-Dee Tweedle-

Dum men attached to a windmill who sawed wood when the wind wished it.

'The town must be further on,' Jack said. 'I think I saw the exit when we came in. It always seems longer when you don't know where you're going.'

Jack drove for twenty-two and one-half minutes and then turned around and drove back. By then the doctor's driveway was empty. Somehow he had rid himself of all his old friends who had just dropped by for a little visit.

They were eating in what Max called his library. Pleasing, Thérèse thought, how the English had such mellifluous names for the commonest of things. That must have been what allowed them to endure Viking invasions and the Blitz, calling an uninspired room with pebbly indoor-outdoor carpeting and some books stacked like cinderblocks against one wall the library. True, it did have a comfortable looking Morris chair of the old sort. Max took that chair. He did not feign genteel hospitality by offering it to anyone else. It was obviously his favourite chair and he had not suffered Royal Medical School and internship and the strictures of socialized medicine not to sit in it. The steel rod in the adjustable back was moved to the last slot, and he was reclined in the chair as if for dental work. In fact he leveled his plate of quiche on his upper thorax, forking it horizontally into his mouth, and his beard worked with his jaw so he could talk and eat and it all looked the same.

'What do you want to know about where you have come to stay for — how long did you say? Only a week? It can't be done, can't be done, cancel your plans, I don't care how pressing your engagements are in wherever it is you think is the centre of the universe — what? Montreal? All right, you have me there, it may well be the centre of one particular universe, a universe in which you are invited to *Portez Vos Vins,* a most civilized custom if I do say so, and I do say so. Nevertheless!'

He held up a fork, a full rest.

'More pie? Help yourselves. As I was saying, I can tell you

what you know and what you need to know and what you don't know you need to know about where it is you find yourselves, aside from being inexcusably under-thirty and, I dare say, in love.'

He stuffed the fork of ham and cheese into his mouth.

'Tell me about the barbed wire,' Jack said. He was sober. He was a good drinker and he was sober. He drained his mug, and refilled it to prove it.

'First you should know,' said Max, 'that I happen to know your predecessor, Mr. Enos Forrest, primarly through his water, which, as the bard says, is first rate, but as for the man who passed the water, he isn't worth a shit. I believe he is living in some plasterboard hutch in town, counting out his days with stacks of dollar bills on the kitchen table. Since he has stopped bringing me samples of his cursed water in a jelly jar, still warm from the tap, so to speak, I don't hear much of him. He thought he had diabetes, because he thought his mother had it. I told him it was liver disease.'

'Did he drink?'

'Did he drink? He would drink this and call it the finest kind.' Max raised his glass and examined the sediment in the bottom. 'The house smelled like a bloody pumpkin half the time. There was always something fermenting under the bed.'

'Why would he put barbed wire in the walls?'

'Second!' Max interjected. 'You should know that Squire Forrest had his reasons for drinking whatever it is you end up with by throwing raisins and brown sugar in a stew inside a pumpkin shell. To wit, he was lonely. He was lonely because he was all alone out there, to which I am sure you can attest. You have been there one night, I understand. It is one of the alonest places on earth, compiled with which was the fact that no one liked the sullen old bastard including myself. He would have twisted the withered arm of his dying mother if he thought it would wring a nickel out of her, and I understand he sold every last thing of hers right down to her Balbriggan drawers at

the auction one at a time, flagging them out in the sun for all
to see and bid upon. But!'

He raised his chin to see over the dish on his chest.

'Who's ready for more?'

Jack held up his hands in protest, and Thérèse was making
hers last by slicing the fork through it in the thinnest pieces. It
was very good quiche, and she was thinking about the joke that
real men don't eat quiche, and it was only a joke, but she was
thinking that real men might not be able to *bake* such a quiche.
There was something extra in it. Mozzarella? Gruyere? Wine?
Beer?

'But! I say he had good reason for his drinking and he is
bloody well rid of the place and, stop me if you don't want to
hear anymore I'm past the point of knowing whether I've gone
too far already or not, you would be bloody well rid of the place
yourselves, as I take it you fully intend to be, and as for the
person or persons who intend to inhabit said domicile, well, I
wish them godspeed and a following wind but I hope they don't
bring me their piss in a jelly jar. God, I do believe I am belly-
up drunk!'

He started to laugh, and it rolled the saucer onto the floor
where it landed harmlessly on the thick carpet.

'It is horrid stuff,' he said, wheezing, 'but God! it gets you
drunk!'

Then he began to cough, and both Jack and Thérèse sat
forward anxiously as always when someone does not know a
person's tolerance for choking. Max waved them back.

'Here now! It is but the mid-day. I have afternoon services to
conduct. I must don the catheter surplice of my office. Eliot
Mayfair, M.D., F.R.C.S., lecturer in tympanic sympathies
and hysterical hysterectomies. To the deuces with your
caduceus. For god's sake, who strapped me to this chair? I've
got a drawer, a whole chest of drawers! Full of pills to push.
Professional sample only. It's a good thing no one else can read.
You know . . . .'

He struggled to sit up in the cushions of the chair and fell back.

'I could be whatever I cared to be if I were that kind of person. You know what I mean? I mean, I could be whatever anyone thought I was. Am I making myself clear? Let me... I'll give you an example. A man comes into my office... sounds like a bloody joke doesn't it? I assure you it's no joke. A man comes into my office, alright, and he's torn the better part of his fifth phalange off with a chain saw. He told me he was reaching out to check the tension on the chain, and he didn't want to bother to shut the bloody motor off. Oh no! too much trouble to flick a tiny little switch no bigger than a fingernail paring. He lets it idle and he reaches out to pull on the chain, and something possesses his other hand to squeeze the trigger of the throttle, something like a feeling that he wants to cut his hand off, maybe, and so he does, almost. Just the one finger, really. Pinkie, to you. So I tell him I can't save the finger, but I can get a nice tuck in the skin and sew it back neat for him so it won't be too horrible looking, and do you know what he says. "Doc, while you're at it, why don't you trim away some of the fat of the hand on that side so it won't be noticed at all." He was serious! "Man," I said! "Man, that's not fat, that's muscle among other things, besides which I am not your meat cutter at the I.G.A." Trim away some of the fat, indeed! You see what I mean. If they wanted me to decide for them which of their sons and daughters to let live, and which to leave out on a cold rock overnight, I could do it. I could! In this day and age! You see ... you see what...'

He was coughing again, and this time he sat up until his head was almost between his knees, and Jack was going to slap him on the back but he waved him away.

'Am I responsible for this?' he said, holding up the mug and letting it drop soundlessly to the resilient floor. 'Forget about a cure for cancer and the common cold. I have found a cure for life!'

'I think you must want us to go,' Thérèse said.

Max wriggled until he was more upright in the chair. He held himself up by the arms.

'I think you must want us to go. That is a sentence construction I cannot make sense of. Let me think on that. I think *you* must want *us* to go. *I* think *you* must want *us* to go. No, I simply cannot get any sense out of that at all. You must be drunk.'

It dawned on Thérèse that he had been drinking before, that he had been drinking while he was getting the quiche ready, that he had been drinking throughout the morning, that he had started the day drinking, that he had never stopped drinking. She was not drunk, Jack was not drunk. The beer was not that strong. It was that horrid but it was not that strong.

Even Enos Forrest had not been that drunk. It was not Enos Forrest that Max was talking about. It was himself.

'I'll tell you,' he was saying, 'I'll tell you plain and simple, but you won't like it. It's plain and simple as the books of local folklore — local folklore, say that quickly fifteen times and see how drunk you think you are — I mean the kind of thing the tourists want. You know. *Tales Out of Old Nova Scotia's Chimneys. Sea Wisdom and Witchery* by Amos Weatherby, R.C.N., Retired. *Ox Yokes and Old Cow Flop.* With coloured photographs that make the daisies stand up and salute, or better yet, black and white so you can see each and every crease on that storm-weathered face. And deep down inside you're thinking, what a quaint old geezer, but I'll bet he's a wife beater, child raper, sheep buggerer, and you're glad he's not your Uncle Teezer. The truth is. . .the truth is! The truth is just as plain and simple as it appears. What those books make the people out to be, what you see them as when you look at them waiting to see me, to let me hack at them or stitch them back together, drop funny little glycerine shells into them I've no god's idea what they do or what they will do fourteen years down the road, bringing me their night's water in a Chum tobacco can, sputum and stool and whatever else their bodies think to squeeze out of them, bringing it to me like a bloody Christmas pudding. They're just what they appear to be. They're just as shallow, shoaled off, benighted, lobotomized, regressed, oxygen-starved as you think they are. Everything you thought they were when you first saw them, they are. Whatever you are thinking, you're right.'

He was breathing with the sound of a huge ancient wheel, and he dropped back and puffed out his cheeks and blew at the ceiling.

'Do you know why Enos Forrest let his farm go for three thousand five hundred dollars? Oh, yes, I know it right to the dollar. Everyone does. It's part of the tourist book truth of the party line and the central operator and one barber in town who went to a hairdresser's convention in Montreal and saw a sign for *douches* and thought it was feminine hygiene. He let it go for next to nothing because he knew that's what it was worth. Next to nothing. Sure we know about your West Germans and the big compounds they're building back in the woods. There's nothing new about that. Canada is full of cowardly bastards like me who run from their homeland. The Dutch are set up with Cadillac dairy farms and automated manure conveyers. The Hindus are right in there with me hacking the fat off the sides of hands to even them up a little. Hell, the Germans are late, man! They're last on the train, with their Land Rovers and their Dobermans and their backwood estates. But you don't see them snapping up a property like the Forrest Estate, do you? And why not? Because somebody told them something, something that even electric fences and guard dogs can't cure. Somebody told them that the people around here aren't worth living near.

'Not that they're dangerous. I don't mean that. They're too bloody stupid to be dangerous. I mean, they simply are not worth being around. Look, would you, if you were a primitive man, say a member of a tribe of Neanderthal man, would you want to associate with another tribe that, say, fed their own body filth to their young, or that knew a way of sticking their

47

tongues up their nasal cavities so they could make their eyeballs pop? I'm just using this as an example, mind you . . . .'

Jack stood up. He did it swiftly and deftly and without a word. He didn't have to say to Thérèse that they were going.

Max rocked, heels off the floor, until he was sitting up with his elbows on his knees. He could not lift his head enough to look them in the eye where they were standing.

'Not going, not going,' he mumbled wetly, something he had worked out of his stomach getting in the way. 'But I haven't told you what it was that bit you today. You want to know why your Mr. Forrest kept barbed wire in his walls. I'll tell you. For the same reason you put buried broken glass and old smashed tins with jagged lids around your vegetable garden. Do you know why? No, of course you don't. You're from the city. Read the tourist book. It will tell you. It's true. Plain and simple. To keep out pests. To keep out the burrowing kind, like cutworms and moles. That's why your Mr. Forrest put barbed wire in his walls. To keep out his neighbours.'

'His neighbours were few and far between,' Jack said coldly.

'Oh, no,' said Max, and he managed to look up from under the tousled white hair, like the beard of an upside-down man. 'You haven't looked close enough. He had a very close neighbour, calling distance away. Just across the lake, the narrow end, by the cranberry bog. It was always shallow there in the summer. They could walk their oxen across to share the plowing. The name was Goetz. You don't see the Goetz farm now when you look out your back door, do you? I wonder why. But it's there. You'll know it when you find it, because there's nothing there. Three things old Enos could see when he looked out his back door. One was the big rock maple, and another was the Big Dipper at night, and the third was the light in the window of the Goetz farm, but now there's only the tree and the star. I wonder why. Do you wonder why? Do you wonder enough to go over there? Or would you rather go back to Rue de la Saint Louis de Ha-Ha and wait for the West Germans to get desperate enough to buy your land? Hmm? I wonder.'

He was facing the floor, staring down at the patternless carpet, when they left.

Jack did not say goodbye. He did not like to see adults helpless. Thérèse felt herself pressed by an old childhood politeness to say something.

'*Merci,*' she whispered, but the first syllable was a soundless breath, and the second was the sound you might make to call a house pet to your side.

The laboured breathing of the doctor, with the wheeze like a grindstone, was his own reply.

They got into the car without speaking. Even with the windows down it had collected a heat that pressed on Thérèse's temples like hard knuckles.

'Can you imagine,' she said, as Jack clattered the key into the ignition, 'that he does this every day?'

Jack did not answer. Before he turned the key, he had to know where he was going.

VI

JACK DROVE INTO THE TOWN OF CLIFTON BRIDGE. IT WAS HALF an hour from the doctor's. It was where the real estate office was, and the bank. Jack said he would drop in on the bank manager, just to introduce himself. It would make dealing easier later if he had to handle it by mail or over the phone. But it was Saturday and the bank was closed. And there was no one in the office of Dominion Realtors when he looked in. Mrs. Berry, who had handled the transaction for him, had her name on a brushed steel plate on a walnut prism on her desk, and she had a spring clothespin, as big as a baby alligator, jaws bursting with papers, memos, receipts, raggedly slit letters. The clothespin was labeled *Mañana*.

Main Street was Queen Street. Jack made a circuit of King Street and Prince Street and Empire Street, and saw the entire business district of the town in a block that would not exercise a dog. He angled into a diagonal parking space behind a pick-up with a black dog hanging his head over the side, and two tow-headed children hanging out the passenger window. He and Thérèse had coffee at a counter in The Smoke Shoppe, which sold candy and magazines. There were five stools at the counter, all vacant. On the wall behind the counter were cup hooks holding mugs with names on them. They were not for sale. They belonged to the regulars. Those who had not been able to find their name already on a mug had stuck it on with a Dymo labeler, or chosen a mug with a unique motto or cartoon. Jack saw Mrs. Berry's mug, he was sure. It was a giveaway Dominion Realtors mug with the company logo. There was an Irving mug and a Home Hardware mug. All the businesses of the town seemed to be suspended on the wall.

'Where is everybody?' Jack asked the girl behind the counter, indicating the mugs.

'Saturday's slow,' she said, setting down the coffee for Jack and Thérèse. 'Friday night's when most everybody does their shopping.'

Jack and Thérèse drank out of styrofoam cups.

In Home Hardware he found everything he wanted. The girl in the red and white blazer packed it for him in a box and he carried it out to the car. Right away he put on the Home Hardware cap he had bought and looked at himself in the mirror. It made him look like he played for a commercial ball team. It made him feel like he belonged. He wanted to go back in and carry out bags of fertilizer and grass seed and long-handled True Temper tools and chuck them into the back of the car behind the pick-up with the kids and the dogs. Thérèse reached behind to steady the box as Jack backed out.

'What do you want all this stuff for? First you tell the man you don't want anything in the house except a bed and a table and chairs, and then you start refurnishing it. We've got all of this already at home, what are we going to do with it when we leave? Coffeepot, tea kettle, frying pan. What is this thing?'

'Egg separator.'

'Egg separator! What do you want to separate an egg for?'

Jack shrugged and looked at himself again in the mirror. He looked cute in the cap.

'I thought it looked neat.'

'Jack, we're not furnishing two complete homes, are we? I thought the idea was to make the investment and then get rid of it.'

'Sure, but I've got to have something in the house so a person can spend overnight, don't I? Us, at least. Or a prospective buyer. I mean, that's all I want the table and chairs for anyway. A place to sign the contract.'

'And the bed?'

'A place to get laid. The first thing a new buyer wants to do is get laid in his own home.'

'Well, you certainly did.' She was following with her fingernail the grain of the padded dashboard.

'I know. You know the first thing somebody told me when they found out I'd bought a place in the country? They said, "Great! You'll love it! You can haul giggy in your own front yard." '

'What does that mean, haul giggy? Wait a minute, I think I know.'

'Sure you do.'

'It's a funny word, isn't it, giggy?'

'It's a funny thing, sometimes.'

'Yes.' She looked at him and smiled. The cap was ridiculous.

He drove across the one-lane bridge. On the other side he

waved two fingers at the driver of the car waiting for him to cross.

'Do you know him?' Thérèse said.

Jack was deep in thought. 'I want a mug with my name on it,' he said.

THEY FOUND A CANTEEN DOWN THE RIVER. THE WALL WAS shingled with a tin Seven-Up sign and an Orange Crush bottle and an ice cream cone as big as a cheerleader's megaphone. They were served fish and chips in cardboard trays on waxed paper placemats. They ate with little wooden forks like toy devil tridents. There was a flavour of ice cream they had not tried before, Grape Nut, and they took cones out to the car. Jack drove with the cone in his left hand. Little BBs crunched in his mouth.

'Do you know where you're going?' Thérèse asked. He had turned upstream.

'Should be simple enough,' he said, bringing the ice cream cone to twelve o'clock when he turned right. 'I'll follow this until we come to another bridge and then I'll cross the river again and we should be back on our own side and we should find our way home.'

'Where do we live?' Thérèse said, unconsciously joining him in acceptance of the new place. 'Is it Clifford Bridge we live in?'

'It's Clifton Bridge, and no, we don't live in Clifton Bridge. I'm not sure where we live has a name. There's no road sign with a name. It must be just the outskirts of something.'

'Well, we must live somewhere.'

He looked at her, and she was intent on the edges of her ice cream cone, peeling the waffled rim back with her teeth, rotating the cone.

'We live in Montreal,' he said, and then added, unfairly, 'Remember?'

BEFORE THEY WENT TO BED, JACK TOOK OUT OF THE GROCERY bag a box of something called Pop Tarts.

52

'You've got to have a toaster for those, dummy,' said Thérèse.

'Do you? I'll get one next time I'm in town.' He handed her the cold pastry with the white icing.

'You would die in the country,' she said, biting into the jelly filling. 'You're so helpless.'

'Am I?' He stood before her and walked her back until he was pressing her against the doorframe at the foot of the stairs. He took the Pop Tart from her mouth and when he kissed her, there were still crumbs on her teeth. He had both his legs between hers, and if she wanted she could lift her feet off the floor and be suspended. When he was this close to her, she thought sometimes that his broad forehead was like the blade of a shovel, like a helmet, because when his mouth was on hers, she could not see his eyes.

'Are we going to haul some giggy?' she said.

'I certainly hope so,' Jack said, lifting her so that she could wrap her legs behind his waist. He carried her that way up the stairs, one hand on the bannister, and her arms were around his neck and she put her head down on his shoulder and she thought this was like what every girl dreams of, being carried upstairs to bed by her father and then marrying him. Of course, it was everyone else's fathers that she had wanted to marry. She did not remember being carried upstairs by her own. She did not remember if the house had even had stairs. But this house was bringing it back to her, giving her something she had missed. She did not blame her father for dying. It was as if he had hired Jack to find her for him which is what he had done: first at the restaurant off Rue St. Denis where they were sitting back to back at different booths eating the same smoked meat sandwiches; then on the empty stage when she came back out after the performance of *Pineapple Poll* to pick up a ribbon she had dropped and he was standing, leaning on the stage, waiting for her; then on the street outside the school in the snow when she knew he was following her. She showed him the shop where her mother had worked. It was still a Chinese novelty store. She bought him black slippers, and she took him back to her apartment and she showed him how they would keep their shape if he put a balloon inflated to the size of a sausage inside each one at night. The next day he moved in. *Anglais.* Face like a shovel. A cologne he used called English Leather that she thought smelled like horse piss. He stayed two years, and then when her company was going to Boston, he married her in the university chapel, his university, and her friends sat on one side, small and lithe, fairies and nymphs, and his friends sat on the other side, bulky and jostling and taking up too much room in the pews, and somehow it had worked, for this year anyway. Some of her friends said marriage would spoil everything, but sometimes, like now, being married to Jack was like dancing. As now her feet were off the ground and he laid her weightlessly on her back on the old metal bed and it jingled slightly in greeting.

She was wearing jeans, as he was, and he unzipped for both of them, and left his slack and tugged hers down. She reached up and behind to hold the headrail. When he pulled on her pants, he lifted her buttocks right off the mattress.

'I feel like a baby being changed,' she said.

She kept her hands there as he pulled down her bikini panties with the same stroking motion over her hips, and then she was wearing only the red plaid shirt she thought of as her cowboy shirt, and he was still pulling down over her hips as if there were more to take off and she had to hold onto the headboard to keep from being pulled off the bed. She felt she was in a strong wind, flying like a flag from the rail. It made her think of movies she had seen in which women have difficult births and their wrists are roped to the bed, and she had always thought the groans and gritted grunts of the women in labour sounded like sexual ecstasy, and she had been able to close her eyes in the theatre and listen to the moment of conception at the moment of birth, the howl of the child a climax.

She released her grasp on the rail when Jack moved his hands under her buttocks and lifted her to him, and she ran her fingers through his hair, from her hair into his hair between her thighs, and curled her fingers behind his ears touching the secret hollow at the back of the earlobe. She combed his hair back and back again, straightening the little waves on either side over the ears in the hair that was black in the dark and almost auburn in the sun after he washed it and was sitting in the kitchen of their apartment, by the one window where the sun came in, and the streaking back of her fingers in his hair made him look as if he were racing into her, as if she were a wind flying around him, then with the muscles of each buttock balled in his hands, and his nose nuzzling up and up like an animal looking for something and kissing sounds from his lips and then his tongue, wide and wet at first, then stiff and pointed like the sodden pointed end of the ice cream cone with cream dripping out that she sucked and at last engulfed and chewed and swallowed, he was making the sound come out of her again. It was a sound like the neck of a balloon squeaking, low and steady at first in the long exhalation of giving up every muscle to this release, then pulsing as muscles shuddering up from the racing in the joint of her Y made her breath stagger, as if she were being shaken roughly by the shoulders on the bed. Then each breath out ended in a gasp, a cry, higher and higher in pitch, arcing up like fingernail cuts on his back, and she was singing, she thought, in a thin, reed-like tone that carried far outside herself and outside the window and across the night. And then, as solidly and surely as the climax was building, it was toppled when she heard something in the cry she made that could not be made by her alone. It was something answering from outside the window. It was harmony. And she locked her knees on the sides of Jack's head and he looked up, and she sat up suddenly against the headboard, drawing her bare legs up against her chest, leaving him crouched at the foot of the bed, holding himself up on his arms, as if he had chased her into a corner. He heard it too.

'What is it?' she breathed. She knew now that it had not been answering her, she had been answering it. The cry continued, the stretched balloon neck, grass blade blown between thumbs, not a human, not a bird.

'It's an animal of some sort,' Jack said, sitting sideways on the bed so he could bring his ear close to the dark screen.

'Don't,' she said, reaching out to bring him away from the window, but she could not reach without moving from where she was pressed at the head of the bed, so she left her arm out, and then it dropped when he pulled further away, trying to see out the screen.

'I don't know, it's a rabbit or a cat or something. Something is supposed to sound like a baby when it cries, what is it? A Siamese cat sounds like that. Is that what it is, a Siamese?'

This was no Siamese cat. The people below them in the apartment had a Siamese. This was no Siamese.

'What is it doing?'

Jack shook his head to silence her, and his hair scraped on the window screen.

'Something I remember from mowing lawns when I was a kid...I heard that....'

Then he remembered, making money mowing lawns with his father's big power mower, self-propelled. You had to lift the rear wheels when you wanted to pull it back, and once he had let it jam itself under a cedar bush by the shady foundation of a house, and he had unleashed that same squawling, and had found a baby rabbit cut open by one swipe of the big rotary blade, its belly sheared grey and slick, like the underside of your tongue, so that you could almost imagine sewing it shut again and turning it loose, except it was making that sound, that piercing oboe shriek, too big a sound to be coming from its body, and the sound was making the guts swell more and more out of the bloodless wound, and he hadn't known what to do, what would stop the sound before somebody discovered. He knew people talked about drowning kittens. There was a bucket by the spigot with the garden hose, and he filled it.

Then he took one of the floppy cotton gloves he used when working around prickly things like ornamental pines, and he pulled it over the rabbit as if tucking it into bed, and he sealed shut the cuff of the glove with his fingers and thrust the rabbit underwater. For a few seconds there was no movement, at least the sound had stopped, and little bubbles were rising from the nap of the cotton, rising like effervescence, then suddenly the glove came alive like a hand severed and horribly animated. It looked like a Mickey Mouse hand cut off and grasping at him, a sorcerer's revenge, and he let go of the cuff and one paw of the rabbit scratched out at him and the head rose, hair matted and eyes bulging, and a big bubble came out of the mouth as if it were spitting up the bubbles of its guts. Jack tried to hold it under the water with his bare hand but it was scratching and biting at him and at last it got past him and the grey, newborn looking glossy muzzle pressed into the air and released a scream of accusation for all the world to hear. Jack upended the bucket, trapping the rabbit underneath in the flood of water, and then quickly flipped the bucket over and fast, so he would not see, smashed the bottom of the bucket down and down and down again on the grey mess until it was quiet. Then in the aftermath, he heard all the hush of the neighbourhood listening, roaring in his ears.

Thérèse was huddled at the end of the bed. He did not know how he could go to her.

'It sounds like something being born,' she said, so it would not hear.

'No,' Jack said, and then again, low, almost a moan, as he drew away from the window, still not able to go to his wife. 'No. Not being born.'

VII

JACK WAS ALREADY UP WHEN THERESE CAME DOWNSTAIRS IN THE morning. She had no recollection of sleeping beside him in the night. She thought they had ended up sleeping back to back, he taking the side nearest the window, she gripping the edge of the mattress as if she might roll off it. It had not been hard sleeping without love, without contact. It had been like it usually was.

He had made coffee in his new coffee pot, a plug-in percolator. It burbled on the counter in the dining room. It was the only sound downstairs.

She went outside to look for him. It gave her a chance to look at the house.

The house appeared to have been flattened by a weight from above. The ridges were bowed, especially that of the woodhouse and the porch. If the house had been three storeys tall, instead of one-and-a-half, it might have looked imposing against the sky. Instead it looked slumped, like an ice cream cake.

A blind ell with no windows was pulling away from the parlour. There was a crack you could slide your hand into between the two walls. It was wet there, and moss was growing on the pine shingles. The ell contained what Jack said was called the birthing room, a downstairs bedroom for giving birth or dying. The linoleum on the floor was worn through in four spots from the legs of the iron bed, now gone, sold at the auction along with the cardboard religious mottoes from the wall. Tres did not like the sightless cell from the inside, it seemed soaked in the sweat of labour and pain. From the outside, it looked like a tumorous growth on the body of the house.

Jack was down by the lake, at the foot of a slope which had spilled the seeds of the perennial garden in the back into wild lupines and black-eyed Susans. Near the shore where Jack stood were pond lilies. They had not blossomed yet. They were green like the scales of something that lay barely submerged in the shallows. Jack did not see her until she called and waved, and then he did not wave back but simply nodded and waited for her to come down to him. She followed his tracks pressed into the tall grass like water spots on velvet.

'North,' he said, pointing across the lake past a marshy peninsula where a lone tree stood, a stunted spruce. 'I checked last night before I went to bed. Before I went *back* to bed. You know what he said about seeing the Big Dipper from the back door. That's north, across there. That's where that place is he was talking about, the Goetz place.'

She was hungry but that was all right, she lived with hunger. But she didn't like the way Jack had gone out without her, not thinking about where they were going to go for breakfast, or what he was going to make if he had brought something in his grocery bag and his rattling carton from the hardware store. She did not like the way he had left just the coffee pot for her, like leaving the cat's dish full for a weekend. She did not like the way he had come down to the lake to look at something without telling her.

If she wanted to be left alone, she could be back in Montreal doing it.

'Uh huh? So?'

'I'm going over there to take a look.'

'Are you? Well, you are stupid. You can't walk on water, you know.'

'I'm not going to. I could walk around through that cranberry bog but I don't have any high rubber boots. I can get some. If I had some hip waders I could do it, but damn it, it's Sunday and everything will be closed, I bet.'

'It was Saturday and everything was nearly closed.'

'Anyway, I'm not going to walk. I'm going to swim.'

He faced back across the lake as if it were the English Channel. It wasn't that far, maybe a quarter of a mile, close enough that you could see there was nothing over there, not a house or a cabin or a dock for the entire length of the lake until it stretched out of sight behind the spruces on this side.

'Why do you want to swim across the lake?' she said.

'Because I want to see where the Goetz farm was, and that's the only way to get there.'

'And why do you want to see where the Goetz farm was?'

'Because that's what he ended up saying, that there was something over there.'

'What he said was that there was nothing over there, nothing left at all, and besides he was drunk.'

'That's why I believe him. I think he told us something he didn't really mean to. I think he may not remember it this morning, and if he does, he regrets it. I want to see what it is.'

'Jack,' she said, controlling herself, taking his arm, 'is this the way it is when you are doing something that is going right for you? I mean, is this what it is like when you think you are going to be the person you want to be when you are thirty-five? Because, if it is, then I'll just stay home the next time. I thought when you did your business you met some people, I don't know, had a few drinks, went out to dinner, maybe a conference in a hotel suite, somebody signing a contract on somebody's back. But if it's you standing at the edge of some lily pads talking about swimming across a lake, I don't have to be here doing this with you, I can be back in . . .'

He shrugged his arm out of her grasp. He was unbuttoning his shirt, the brown-striped one. Before, she had always seen it with a tie. Seeing it open at the throat, and now him pulling the tail out of his jeans, she thought of a man undressing before he kills himself so he will not spoil his good clothes, and she took the shirt from him.

'You can stay here and watch me, or you can go back to the house and have some coffee and wait for me, or you can drive wherever and have waffles and French toast for all I care, or you can go back to flaming Montreal. Yes! This *is* what I do!'

He had stripped to his jockey shorts. He still wore the white ones, although she had asked if she could buy him some coloured ones, skimpier, sexier. He had a good body. Black briefs would look good on him. The little pot of a belly looked like a hibernating animal inside him, and when he straightened you could scarcely see it.

'Are you a good enough swimmer?' she said, seeing that he had now stepped into the mud at the edge, the cold water making the hairs on his shins bristle.

'He said it was shallow at this end. He said they used to drive their cattle across.'

'That was in the summer, when the water was low.'

'This is the summer.'

'Is the water low?'

'*I* don't know! I don't know, do I? All right?'

'I'm not a good swimmer,' she said, her feet twitching, toes rippling inside the soft sneakers.

'I'm not asking you to come with me.'

'I'm not staying here,' she said, starting to unbutton her blouse. He watched, as if he did not believe her, until she was naked.

'Take off those stupid underpants,' she said.

She waded in to join him, repeating to herself 'This is stupid, stupid, stupid.'

It was not shallow where they entered. At waist depth, the water at their feet became suddenly colder, then the bottom fell away. They had passed through the lilies, tendrils twining around their legs as if searching for a hold, and now they leaned forward and planed across the clear water and swam north.

They would pass close to the jut of the peninsula. Maybe there it was shallow and they could stand up if they needed to rest. They spoke of this as they swam side by side, keeping their heads out of the water so they could see and talk. Jack did a kind of breast stroke, and Thérèse swam on her side facing him.

Once she said, 'If I can't make it, will you hold me up?' and he looked scared and said 'Can you make it?' and began to swim harder, to get them both there.

'Can you touch?' she said, water running into her mouth, when they were far enough out that going back was no solution.

He bobbed and disappeared under the water and came back up with an answer in a burst of pent air. 'No!'

She thought of herself as too light to swim well. She could not float to rest. Her feet sank if she tried to float on her back. Jack could do it. He showed her how, sculling water with his hands. It was like battleships, she thought. Battleships were heavy, so they could float. She was too light, so she could not float. They even made boats out of concrete. It didn't make sense, but here was proof that that was the way it was. She had to work all the time, like a hummingbird with a heart beating a million times faster than anything else's.

She pulled ahead of Jack with her steady side-stroke, and she angled slightly toward the point of land. She did not want him to see this. He would make her stay out in the middle going north, but she was thinking about where she would go when she felt the exhaustion make her sick to her stomach and then she would gag on some water and she would flounder and there would be only a few more seconds she would have to get to shallow water. She had told him she was not a good swimmer. It was not what a dancer could do. Her muscles were trained to play with gravity. This was weightlessness, but it was failing. It was like trying to learn to fly while falling.

'Hey!' Jack said, twisting around from his back to see her ahead of him, and just then, as if to prove that she was leading him, she felt something under her feet, something scraped the side of her lower leg, and it was not the shallows of the peninsula.

Her legs recoiled instinctively. It had felt like dragging her legs over the back of a whale suddenly close in the depths of the ocean. She did not know what it was, but she knew not to trust it. Then her knee hit it again and she had to stop stroking the water to reach down and put her hand over the scrape, and her body sank just enough so that she was sitting sidesaddle, her chin just out of the water, on a big rock.

Jack drew closer, and still he did not know that she was not floating. She let her toes explore the carapace of the rock, and she found that it slanted upward from all sides, like the tip of a pyramid, and she was near the top. She hunched herself higher up the rock, her feet pushing against the sloping sides which were not mossy or slimy but rough like concrete on an unfinished floor. Just as Jack was close enough to see that she was not treading water, she stood up before him, shedding silver splashes in his face. She was ankle deep in the middle of the lake.

He backpaddled, squinting up at her against the water running from his brow, and he whistled and grinned.

'Whew! Have you found something! How big is it?'

To show him, she paraded around the rounded tip of the pyramid, an area no bigger than a table for two in an intimate cafe. Then her feet slipped off the steeper side and she slid up to her neck again, flailing in the water, but triumphant.

Jack sat on the rock and pulled Thérèse up beside him. By scrunching their knees together, they could both sit on the top, high enough out of the water that the sun was warming them. The rock was rough against their bare skin, but it did not seem as if they were naked, because they were so close beside each other. And it did not seem as if they were exposed because there was clearly nobody else around. They had ended up facing the house.

'I wonder what it looks like from the shore,' Jack said.

'It looks like two pond sprites sitting on a lily pad,' Thérèse said, pressing her shoulder against his, enjoying his warmth.

'Fantastic!' Jack swung around, looking at the north shore,

his movement almost sliding him off his perch. Thérèse held onto him until he had twisted around to see where they were going. 'Can you make it the rest of the way?'

'Of course,' she said, 'now that this friendly hippo or elephant or brontosaurus or whatever he is has been good enough to give me the loan of his back for a little while.'

She slipped back into the water and paddled ahead. Jack followed her, and before he had gone many strokes, he turned back to get a sighting that would let him find the rock again, but it was gone, there was no evidence of it beneath the water. He set his sights on a clump of white birches on the north shore.

THE BOTTOM, WHEN THEY FOUND IT, WAS MUDDY, AND LAYERED with dead leaves, like a sunken, spoiled library. Sloshing through the muck to the grassy bank left them bruised with brown slime from the knees down, and as soon as Jack stood in the clammy shade of the trees, he did not want to be there. He wanted to be back on his own side, in the sun. It would be noon, or later, before the sun fell on this side.

Thérèse had gone ahead of him, through the marshy grass and the birches and willows along the bank, looking for a sunny clearing. The mud on her legs was streaked like fine hairs, and he followed her rolling hips and plunging thighs as if following game into the bush. He shielded his groin with a hand as he went through the tall grass.

The clearing showed just the slightest slant of sun on the tops of the trees. It was still cold and in shadow on the ground. It was as if someone had laid a flashlight at the lip of a well, shining across it like a bridge. Jack felt the coarse mat of lichen under his feet, dried tight fibres like something you would use to scrub out a pot, and he knew only that nothing seemed to be growing here, and then he knew that he had found what was left of the Goetz farm.

'He said there was nothing.'

The ground seemed scourged, burned, blackened even to the grated, shaled shell of rock that showed through in places between the packed clay earth and the tough mat of lichen. The clearing was not large but he knew that perimeter was deceiving, especially with buildings, which had so much of their existence in the air. He tried to imagine a house and barn in the clearing then a kitchen garden, maybe a potato piece. Where was the pasture for the cattle? Where was the plowed ground? He decided that over the years the trees had closed in. Just beyond the ring must be more cleared land. These were the weeds of the woods, birches and willows and alders. They could have grown up in ten or twelve years. And how long had the farm been vacant? Max had not said. And what did old Mr. Forrest have to worry about so long after the farm was vacant, anyway?

There were no answers. Jack had found exactly what he had been told he would find. Nothing.

He stood in the centre of what he thought had been the foundation, a dished place, but there were no stones, no timbers fallen and rotting, no corner posts. And somehow he knew there would be nothing if he dug down, either, not that the soil seemed to permit any excavation. The most he could do with his fingers was prise off onion layers of brittle crust. And it was not comfortable for sitting on, either. Both Jack and Thérèse were standing in the middle of the clearing, she shivering now, and now he felt naked, now he felt exposed, watching the clock of the sun's shadow creep down the tree trunks, and the quivering wafers of a beech like gold coins spilling, forever spilling down, but nothing was collected.

IT SEEMED WARMER IN THE WATER. THEY WERE HALFWAY BACK across when they heard the singing down the shore. It came to them in a gust of freshening breeze, between strokes in the water, and they both stopped for a second time to listen. It came again. Singing, in unison, mostly women, high shrill nasal voices, almost keening, but a song that made you think of comraderie, like a drinking song. Jack couldn't place it, couldn't make out the words with his head bobbing in the water.

'Make for the big rock,' he gasped.

They tried to find it. He let Thérèse go ahead, in unspoken acknowledgement that she had found it first. He was sighting behind him at the clump of birches, and across to the house, and he knew that the rock lay just below the surface, but it neither rippled the water nor darkened it.

The singing seemed louder, as if the voices were coming closer, or were coming out of cover. Jack glanced over his shoulder in mid-stroke, expecting to see the people somewhere along the shore, but he could not, although he could almost pinpoint the place the voices were coming from. Between two peach coloured boulders on the bank.

He had drifted away from Thérèse, thinking the big rock was more in the middle, and she was angling toward the boggy point of land, and he knew that in their searching they would be using up energy that should be carrying them toward shore. He didn't know exactly why he wanted to find the rock, except that he could rest on it and try to see where the singing was coming from, and also maybe to hide behind it. He was thinking of the jokes about skinny-dippers being caught by a tour of bird-watchers. He did not think that they should keep swimming for home, that their nakedness would not be seen underwater. He did not, in fact, think that he could make it to the shore. And in a minute, nakedness was not going to matter. He turned desperately toward Thérèse, cutting toward the peninsula, just as he found that his shoulders could not lift his arms to stroke anymore, and then his knee crashed into the point of the rock, and he lay upon it, belly down, and breathed and tried to call to her.

She had heard him stop, and had turned already. She swam

up strong, though her legs were low in the dark water. She swam onto the rock like a boat entering a slip. Neither of them spoke. From here they could see the people.

VIII

THEY HAD COME OUT OF THE TREES BETWEEN THE TWO BOULDERS, and their words were clear now:

'How glad I am,
How glad I am,
Since Jesus washed
My sins away.'

The women sang as one of them was led into the water by a man in a black suit, white shirt and tie. The woman, or girl, was draped in a shapeless grey raincoat, to protect her modesty when she came out of the water and it pressed her dress against her figure. There were men in black suits as well, and their voices were a low grumbling under the tune, as if they were a motor driving it.

'How glad I am,
How glad I am!'

The man in black in the water tipped the woman over backward, a handkerchief held to her nose, and brought her right back up, and led her back to shore where the other women reached out to her.

'How glad I am!'

'Do you hear that?' Jack whispered from his hiding place at the big rock, clinging to it like a barnacle with Thérèse, just their heads from their chins up showing out of the water, two heads spotted in the water halfway out if anyone had cared to look there.

'That tune. Do you know what it is?' He sang it for her hurriedly, softly. 'How dry I am, how dry I am, nobody knows how dry I am!'

The next woman was wading into the water on the hand of the man. His pant legs were wrapped around, like a wet flag on a pole in the rain. She went out waist deep and lay back and submerged, and Jack sang softly,

'How dry I am,
How dry I am,
Nobody knows
How dry I am.'

He was starting to laugh, shivering too from the cold of staying still in the water, and Thérèse was worried that they would be heard, seen, in their hiding place which was no hiding place at all behind the unseen rock. It was just a place to hold themselves in midstream, a place where no one would expect to see a couple of heads looking back at them, or poor eyes would mistake them for a pair of ducks or loons. But they could not start swimming again now, for the celebrants were all on the shore, facing out across the lake, almost directly across from the house, so they had to stay in the water up to their noses, like anchored decoys. She started to laugh. Loons was right.

Three more women were baptized, no men, and each time Jack sang his words to their tune as if he had not made the irony clear to Thérèse. She had not heard the song before, neither his nor the Baptists', and it did not seem so extraordinary that one tune would have several different uses. It was an especially grating tune, though, monotonous, uninspired, and she was getting sick of it.

As if to entertain her, after the last dunking and the preacher dragging his dripping suit and his squelching shoes out of the water onto the little pebble beach, Jack said, 'Watch this!' and crouched and then stood up in full view on the topmost piece of the rock. Now Thérèse was hidden, hidden behind her husband who was naked full front to the Sunday gathering on the shore.

He stood rigid, one hand lifted toward them. He had made scarcely a sound pulling himself upright, so no one had looked out on the water. Their eyes were on the preacher, who had taken a stand on a flat rock in front of them, and who was starting to lead them in another hymn. But this one did not get far enough to become boring.

'Are you washed,
Are you washed . . .'

Then someone saw, someone whose gaze drifted across the water in lazy recess from the service and fell upon the upright white body of the mature male standing upon the water.

The singing fell to silence, like silt settling. And Jack took the opportunity of having their undivided attention by beckoning to the faithful to come to him across the water, walk to him, O ye of little faith. He drew his lily white palm again and again toward himself.

Thérèse watched from between his feet, her prune wrinkled fingers clutching the rock. There was a frozen moment.

Then hub-bub.

The faithful abandoned the shoreline amid shrieks and screams of irreversible violation and the voices of the men were like axes clopping into hollow wood. The voices continued into the trees and along the shore until it became evident that they were heading for the blasted clearing of the old Goetz farm where they could have a closer look at the source of the sacrilege. The very tree tops seemed to shake with vengeance at their passing. Jack and Thérèse swam for the home shore, their feet splashing behind them in a spray that hid their white bottoms, and by the time the angry mob had reached their closer vantage point, Jack and Thérèse had found their clothes and were stealing, crouching, through the tall grass back to the house. They reached the back door still unclothed and ducked inside. Their bare legs were stuck with seeds of the grasses.

Jack was jumping up and down on the linoleum, shaking his fists in voiceless glee as if they still had a reason to stay quiet. He took Thérèse by the shoulders and made her dance with him, bouncing on the floor, almost weightless. Her eyes dropped to see the floor spring away, and she saw something else bobbing up and down between them as they jumped. It was impressive in its supple rigidity, joining them between them like a jealous child.

'Did you have that when you stood up?' she asked him, and he looked down and the erection looked back.

'Gee, I don't think so.'

They both looked at it as if it were a marvel.

'Cold water usually makes me small,' Jack said.

'What is it that make you big?' she said, moving against him, her hand taking the proffered part of him as if in greeting.

Jack answered without hesitation.

'Success.'

She held the cold, firm, fish hardness, and then the truly marvelous thing happened. It shrank from her grasp, escaped her completely, melted out of her hand, and lay slack against his inner thigh, and they both looked down at it until it was no longer interesting. Then they dressed.

THEY HAD THE COFFE JACK HAD MADE. HE WANTED TO MAKE French toast in his new frying pan but the stove had been sold.

'Next time I'll buy a hotplate,' he said.

Thérèse made rosettes of the tomatoes Jack had bought, using his new paring knife that came on a cardboard display package with a picture of tomato rosettes. And they had the last of the Pop Tarts cold. Jack talked about the type of toaster he would buy, one that had different shades of tan on the dial to show how dark your toast would be. They did not talk about his marvelous shrinking erection. It was understood that it was a phenomenon of the hunt and the chase and muscle contraction and body temperature. And it was understood that this time of the day was not the time to use it anyway.

The knock on the screen door startled them both, and Thérèse was instantly glad they had not gone back to bed, or worse yet, started something on the dining room table. The knock sounded alien in the house that had so far only hosted noises made by them. It also sounded like the end of something. It was the beginning of visitors, and the end of immunity, like moving into a new apartment with a new phone number before the telephone sales campaigns find out your name.

It was the preacher from the water. He was in a dry suit now.

Thérèse stayed behind her husband, chagrined. She felt like a little girl about to be scolded, and she guessed before she heard his voice that he would be Irish, from his split potato nose and pockmarked cheeks. Irish was as bad as British when it came to being chastised.

'I'm Pastor Loomer,' he said, still blocked in the doorway. 'Greetings in Christ, I'm your new neighbour from up the hill.'

Could it be that he did not recognize them from the water? Or at least Jack?

Jack seemed to think so, or at least he was playing it dumb, shaking the man's hand, introducing Thérèse.

'Théresa,' said the pastor, thinking of saints.

'Tres,' Jack corrected him.

'Milford. You've not got family in Glace Bay?'

Jack shook his head and held his wife against him in an uncharacteristic way. 'Tres and I drove down from Montreal for a little visit.'

'You're not...I thought....' The pastor seemed confused. Then he answered himself. 'Summer folk!'

'That's it,' Jack said, too brightly.

'Well, greetings neighbour, even if it is for only the summer. There's still time for you to find yourself welcome to our little place of worship. I came to invite you to this evening's service.'

Jack fumbled. 'My wife is...I don't know, and I'm...I don't know, an agnostic, I suppose...'

The pastor held out his hands to show they were empty. He still had not got inside the door, though the toes of his shiny black brogues were over the sill.

'We minister to the Greek and the Roman as well. I am not here to proselytize, I am here as a good neighbour. You have been open with me, I want to be open with you.'

He gave the slightest wink to Thérèse when he said this. It was not lost on Jack, who stepped back and let the man in.

'I guess open is the word to describe it,' Jack said.

'Fully openhearted and naked in God's company! I daresay you would have had several of my flock following you across the water except for one thing.'

He leaned close to Jack's ear, but his eye was on Thérèse.

'Jesus would have been circumcised!'

His laughter was like a bag of apples spilled on the stairs, and he did not stop until he had found each one of them and stopped them from rolling away.

'I've often thought of that rock, myself,' he said. 'I used to see the boys swim across and stand on it. I used to think, if a church can be founded upon a rock, surely I can found something upon that rock, too. But you've beat me to it, Jack Milford, and I don't blame you a single bit for doing what you did.'

'What boys?'

'I should imagine you're coming here from the big city, you're probably thinking this is the end of the world, and then to see a baptism right out of the Sunday school books, you must have thought it was a laughable thing.'

'What boys do you mean?'

'Ah, but, really what I wanted to come by to tell you was something I didn't want you thinking. I didn't want you thinking that we were doing it only for the entertainment, you must understand. We may be poor simple folk, just country people, but we were doing it because we believed in it. It may have been a comical thing to you, but it was a blessed thing for us.'

His eyes were moist. The Irish, thought Thérèse, weeping at a melody or a piece of black felt. Blowing each other up with car bombs, but sniffling at the cadence of a verse.

'Yes, but what boys did you mean?' Jack insisted.

'What boys when?' The pastor brushed a glimmer out of his eye with the screw of a knuckle.

'Swimming across the lake.'

'Oh, the Goetz boys. From the old farm that was over there. I don't suppose you know about it.'

'Sit down, Mr. Loomer,' Thérèse said, pulling out one of the chairs from the table, and he found that the two of them were already seated, waiting for him.

'I DON'T MEAN TO BELITTLE THE GOOD THAT DR. MAYFAIR HAS done for the community,' the pastor was saying, 'but I do think he should have said nothing at all about those not present to speak in their own defense, rather than give you all kinds of false ideas and impressions with half-truths and innuendos. The doctor has his weakness, as do we all, I warrant you. We all cope with our sorrow in a different way. The doctor copes with his in his way, and pity it is you had to be witness to it your first visit here. The truth is, the Goetz family wasted away out of bad luck and ignorance, neither of which you can blame a man for if he's born into it. I suppose that's what poor people like me are here for, to help those born into poverty and ignorance. Sometimes we just can't do enough.'

His eyes were misty again and they waited for him to continue. He had finished the last of the coffee and the tomatoes and had accepted the cucumber slices with salt that Thérèse offered him, and now there was nothing to hold him except the end of his tale.

'The truth is, they were thought by some to be witches.'

'By some, including Mr. Forrest?'

'I'm sure. And what's worse, they believed it themselves. This community was rife with it when I first came here. It wasn't just the light of the Gospel that was needed. It was three hundred years of civilization. When I first came in 1948, there were roads that couldn't be traveled for three months in the spring for the mud that swallowed you up. And a team of oxen was a man's most prized possession, followed by his rifle, followed by his family name, and somewhere down along with the chickens came his wife. I knew of men who rubbed the same liniment they'd used on their ox on their women, and they worked them like that, too, but the land was that kind of land. It was twisted with roots and stumps, and what they cleared grew right back in if they didn't keep at it year after year after year. Even so, it seemed to creep in around the rocks they couldn't move until there was a little sapling there and they didn't bother to cut it, and the next year it was a small tree and it wasn't doing anybody any harm, and the next year it was a shade tree that the cattle could stand under. You see them still in the fields. Dots of trees around the rocks they couldn't move, a monument to their weakness. Not weakness, humanity.

'If they could hunt, they hunted, but what they didn't catch, they couldn't eat, and sometimes they shot each other instead when they were back in the woods, either by accident or by design, nobody ever knew, because if you couldn't find the deer or the moose, and you weren't going to bring home porcupine for the woman to skin like a squaw, then you might as well shoot somebody else.

'So it worked back up the line, through the family name to the rifle, and finally somebody had to shoot somebody else because of somebody else who'd got shot sometime long ago. You'd think for such a shooting lot, they'd have made fine soldiers, but in both wars when the time came for the country to ask them to do their deed, they looked at the country and they said "I've got my own troubles."

'You know, there were bodies never found? And the first year I lived here, I never trusted to drink from my well. Some of us kept a trout in the well, so you could see if it was poisoned. It's true! I'm telling you, it was the deepest pit of ignorance since the Dark Ages. And if one family was living a little bit apart from everybody else, then people got to thinking there was something queer about them, and they began to treat them that way, and that would make you start acting queer, even if only to get a rise out of them. After a while, it got so you couldn't tell the difference yourself.'

'What kind of queer?'

'Old Man Goetz thought he could put a spell on you. He thought if he wanted something to happen to you, he could make it happen. You take that, and a mean, tight man like Enos Forrest who'd steal the pennies off his mother's eyes, God forgive me but it's true, and the two of them just naturally made trouble for each other.

'Enos had a boil on his leg that wouldn't heal, and I guess he figured it was Old Man Goetz doing it to him, for something he'd done back to him some time ago, something about sharing a team of oxen, I would imagine, which would have been more risky than sharing a wife back then. You would never think you were getting your fair share of it.

'So Enos believed that if he burned a chicken, a live chicken I'm telling you now, burned it alive in his cook stove, and then climbed on the roof and poured a pot full of his own urine down the chimney, the next man to walk through his door would be the one who was witching him.'

'And the next man who did walk through that door was Old Man Goetz bringing back a turnip hoe he had borrowed and had broke the handle. There must have been an awful smell in the house that day but it was nothing like the smell in the Goetz house when they finally found all the bodies.

'There was no telephone through the country then. No way for people to check on them. And, like I said, nobody would have missed them anyway. The only one who would have noticed whether they were coming and going, alive and well, in their own yard, was Enos Forrest and his crippled up mother who couldn't even drag herself to the window to look out. So he never said anything, and nobody thought about them at all until it came time for someone to dig a new well, and he went looking for one of the Goetz's to witch the well for him, because they all could witch water, I know that. I've seen them do it with an alder twig, and they can tell you how deep your well is too. The poor fellow who walked in on that mess! One awful mess it was!

'A solid lead slug from the shotgun to the head of each one of the three boys and the old lady and the old man too, so you had to wonder how it was done, and who had done it to himself last, or if they had each done it to themselves, though they were scattered throughout the house as if they had been roused out of sleep in the night, maybe were running from something . . . .'

'Didn't anyone suspect Mr. Forrest?'

'He had nothing to gain. He wasn't going to murder a whole family over a boil on his leg. No, they just knew what he would say, and I guess the knowing of it got too much for them, so they finished it, though like I say no one will ever know exactly how they did it. Myself, I think it was the father. I can hear him saying to his family, Well, we are going to be declared as witches by Enos Forrest and no one will ever believe otherwise, so damn them all anyway, I hope they like the mess we leave behind!

'As it turned out, there was nothing to do but burn it to the ground, you know. I understand that some of the windows were right solid with the stuff blasted out of them. Not a pane broken, either. And a couple of them must have taken it through the neck, because they lived long enough to drag themselves around in a bloody trail until they were finished, curled up, I understand, like a dog hunting his own tail before he goes to sleep. And they had swollen, some say, like a sack of old potatoes gone bad in the cold cellar, so when you touch it the rottenness spills open.

'Burn it. That was the only thing. Let the Constable take as much of what was left of the bodies to do whatever the law required before burying them, and burn the rest.'

'That explains why nothing grows there,' Jack said.

'They say the fire put heat into the rocks of the foundation that lasted until the first snow, and there was a melted circle inside where the walls had been. And they had been shot early in the fall, because it was still warm enough for the flies to do their job on them.'

'I don't understand why I didn't find the foundation,' Jack said. 'Nothing that looked like a foundation to me, anyway.'

'Split granite. Hauled there by ox team.'

'Nothing.'

'You didn't look.'

'I looked. I got down on my hands and knees and I even scratched at the soil a bit. Nothing except rocks peeling away and that rough, dry moss like a scale, like rust.'

The pastor was alert, as if he suspected Jack was playing a joke on him.

'You didn't go to the old Goetz place.'

'I did. After we swam over and we found the big rock, we

walked all over it, in the clearing. We did.'

The pastor looked at the man's wife, whose lips were white from the details of the story.

'Little clearing, trees all around, topsoil worn away, rough and scabby, nothing growing there?'

He was looking at the wife, but the man answered.

'Yes.'

'You didn't go to where the house was,' said the pastor standing by his chair. He held onto it. 'You went to where they buried the bodies.'

Jack and Thérèse watched him steady himself with the chair, and then he made for the doorway, as if the air in the room were oppressing him.

'But why does nothing grow there?'

'I don't know. I don't go to that place. I only go to that side of the lake when we have baptisms, and the path through the woods leads by the old foundation, and things grow there.'

'But why not . . . ?'

'I don't know! I haven't seen!'

'I have,' Jack said.

The man looked suddenly older, smaller, his stiff shirt collar too big for him, and when he turned his back, the wrinkles in his neck formed a perfect diamond, and there were hairs on the fringe of his ears highlighted by the sun outside the porch door. He spoke without turning.

'I have a wife, children, daughters, one of them is married, she married a schoolteacher and they moved to Winnipeg. One of them is home, yet, due to graduate from grade twelve this coming June. Daughters . . . are hard to keep. Keep. Safe.'

He turned and he worked his face into a shine like the toes of his shoes. 'If I don't see you before you go back, Christ be with you, summer folk!'

They watched him through the window in the ell going up the hill and out of sight. He had walked all the way over from his house in his good suit and polished shoes.

'He is the perfect definition of nutso,' Jack said.

'Did you hear how...excited he got when he was giving us all those gory details?'

'And what was that about keeping his daughters safe?'

'The guy is a wacko,' Jack said, looking up the hill. 'Do we attract them, or what?'

Thérèse turned from the window, turned too quickly, and the lack of food made her light-headed, and in the hollow parlour stripped of everything that had ever been soft and touched by a human hand, she forgot for a dizzying moment why they were here in this emptiness.

'Maybe it isn't us,' she said, when she had found her balance. 'Maybe it's the place.'

'Come on!' Jack said, taking her hand firmly and leading her out of the room.

'Where are we going?'

'When does your plane leave?'

'Not till Friday. Why?'

'I'm driving you to Halifax. If we can't get you on a plane straight away, you can stay in a hotel until the next one.'

'Jack! Stop it!'

He stopped tugging at her.

'What about you? The house?'

He feigned calm, rubbing his hands over the legs of his jeans.

'Maybe I'll fly back with you as well.'

'Your vacation...'

'We'll find a nice restaurant in Halifax, if there is such a thing. It's...yes...what we've been eating...it's...something we've eaten. We've got to get some proper food into our stomachs.'

'Jack, if it's just a meal you want, we don't have to drive all the way to...'

'I want to get out!' His fists were balled on his thighs. 'I want *us* to get out.'

79

'All right, all right,' she said, sliding sideways from him. He was like a powerful child. 'I thought you wanted to stay, but all right, we'll go . . . .'

She let him move past her, and when his hand was on the screen door, just when it touched the wooden crosspiece painted a dun colour, the careless brush sealing up the mesh of the screen nearest it as well, just as his fingers touched the wood, like an alarm the telephone rang.

'Oh, God,' she heard him gasp.

'Did you have the phone connected? I didn't know you . . .'

'I didn't. God, what is it now?'

He didn't even know where the phone was. He followed the strident, tireless alarm, two long rings, four short, to the wall with the china closet and the glass doors.

The phone was a hand-crank model, a walnut varnish, looking like something that should set off dynamite charges.

'It's a Magnetophone,' he said, looking at it. 'God knows what might have made it ring. A thunder storm somewhere.'

'Answer it.'

'Answer . . . who? Who do you expect it to be if it's a thunder storm? God?'

He picked up the receiver. It was the doctor.

'Dreadfully sorry. I have an aunt, you see, who works the central switchboard, and I took the liberty of having her ring you for me. I know you didn't intend to have your service connected for your stay but I assure you things are done much differently in the country, don't you see? And it's only because I wanted to catch you before you went out for a bite to eat. Have you eaten? Well, of course supper I mean. Good. Then I still have a chance to redeem myself after my frightful behaviour of yesterday noon. Do come for supper. I promise to make amends for everything.'

Jack found it hard to make a sound come out of his throat. It was hard talking to God.

'We were just leaving for . . .'

'I do think you'll enjoy it. There's something I do with a Cornish game hen that I think is frightfully clever if I do say so myself, and I do. And I have some very old, very well behaved brandy that is guaranteed to keep me on my best behaviour. None of this homemade stuff. I have chucked the lot of it out. What do you say, when shall I expect you?'

'We were just leaving...for the airport. Just...as you called.'

The line hummed. Jack had an absurd idea that the voice was connected to the hand crank and if he twirled it, the voice would continue like a Jack in the Box. The voice startled him, then, when it continued on its own.

'Look, I dearly want you to come. Besides, I think there's someone here you'll want to meet.'

The line hummed again, and this time it was Jack's voice that had to continue.

'Who is it?'

'Just a moment.'

There was the sound of the receiver being passed over, and some muffled, distant discussion, a hoot of laughter, and then a voice.

'Mr. Jack Milford! Kiddo, you are going to be a very, very wealthy man, and I am the woman you have to thank for it. You get your buns over here!'

It was a voice that could only belong to Berry.

IX

AMY BERRY WAS FROM PALO ALTO AS SHE WAS FOND OF REMINDING anyone who would listen. She had taught creative writing at Palo Alto State Teachers College. Then she had been invited to the Nova Scotia Teachers Summer School where she had hyped her book *Springboards!: Fifty Ways to Get Writing Going.*

'I used to tell my students, write about what you know, and you know, funniest thing, I got up here to Nova Scotia and I looked around and I asked myself, What do I know? And you know what I answered myself? Sweet fuck all! Hell, I been dodging the cactus for pretty near fifty years all along thinking some man was going to come along and take care of me. You know what I said to myself when I looked around here at your lobster fishermen and your logging men and your sweet jeezly big farmers with a milk pail in each hand? I said, hell sweet dildo woman! Ain't no man gonna take a look at you! You're a goddamn dyke! Forget about getting fucked and start thinking about getting rich. That's when I got into real estate and I ain't had a single regret since.'

They were sitting in Max's library again. Amy Berry was squatting on the sofa beside Jack, her belly, or what he assumed to be her belly, between her legs, her arms, elbow bent, hands on knees, as if she were a football linesman. She was wearing what looked to be designer overalls in pink denim.

Max was in his favourite chair, not reclined so far back this time, Thérèse was relieved to see. He was smoking from a calabash pipe, the trumpet bowl orange as a gourd. Thérèse had felt a liquid loosening in herself when he had taken the pipe out of a chamois pouch after dinner to go with the brandy. She had been thinking how much she liked the smell of a pipe. Jack would not smoke one. If he smoked anything ever, it was a cigar. He said a pipe was a time-waster's toy, and cigarettes burned down too fast. If you wanted to smoke something, let it be something that burned untended for half an hour.

But Max's tobacco smelled like he had lit the hairs on his wrist. Thérèse moved away discreetly to the far side of the fireplace, the hearth of which was stacked with books and journals with slippery slick covers. She was sitting on the floor, on the carpet which was like Astro-Turf, or what the people in

Toronto suburbs put in their backyards instead of grass around their pools.

The brandy was good. It had orange blossoms in it, and after she tipped her nose into the snifter, the viscous fluid weeped, clear and sadly like a precious body oil, back into the bowl. The brandy made the occasion an occasion, Amy said.

'Sure, I know I ain't talking about mega-bucks,' she was saying to Jack, 'but I am talking about a 300 per cent increase on your dollar investment. I'm talking about putting your money up in the five-figure bracket which ain't exactly whistling Dixie if you can think of something you'd rather be doing with ten-thousand-five-hunnerd than letting some fat-ass Wop rubber-tire man sit on it while he thinks of somewhere else to spend it. It's some kind of Dago tire company, they make racing tires or something, I don't know, and they want a place they can put up their executives when they're relaxing from a day inspecting the inner-tube plant or whatever it is in Brampton.'

'Brampton, Ontario? And they want a summer retreat in Nova Scotia?'

'Jet helicopters, kiddo! Wake up to it!'

'Then they can afford a hell of a lot more than ten-five.'

'Look, amigo. I ain't saying what they can afford. I is saying what they are willing to pay, which is two different pieces of meat, if you catch my drift. I just got wind of it last week, and when I heard from the sawbones here that you were in town, I thought I'd lay it on you. You sound like a man who doesn't mind making a fast buck. Pleasure doing business with you. You want to think it over, think it over. You want to talk it over with the little woman, talk it over. But, I'm telling you, the money is there.'

Perched as she was on the points of her knees, her short black hair swept back over her ears, she looked as if she were riding herd on something.

She jutted her chin at Thérèse. 'What about it, darling? You fancy going home with ten grand in your pocket and an extra five hunnerd for a dirty weekend in the city of your choice?'

Thérèse sat straighter, to ease the cramp in her back. It had come from sleeping on the saggy mattress, she was sure. Tonight she would get Jack to put the mattress on the floor. At home they had a *futon*.

'What about these Germans...' Jack began.

Amy twisted her head back and forth as if at a slow-learning cow pony. 'Shit. You want to sit around and wait for the mega-bucks to roll in when the Reds get their act together or you want to move now?'

'It's not a lot of money.'

'I'm not talking about ten-five in your pocket! I'm talking about ten-five you can make do something for you! Don't tell me you can't think of something it can do for you. What's your business? Computers?'

'Educational software.'

'Hell, man! I knew you were for me! I found out about the bucks in education myself at an early age, right about soon as I got out of school. I said to myself, "Like taking candy from a baby, like taking candy from a baby!' Shit. Ten-five'll get you the best hooker in town in any city outside of maybe Teheran where they breed them to be virgins, never take the veils off, use them once and throw them away. All it takes is a set-up with your Education Minister and you're in with Flynn.'

'Yeah, okay...' Jack smirked nervously, looking at the ceiling.

Amy mimicked him. 'Yeah, okay, gee golly, I dunno... What are you waiting for, the crops to come up? What do you think you're going to do with that property when you leave here? The next thing you're going to hear is that somebody torched the house, but that's no great loss, because they'll bulldoze the thing anyway. And then you'll hear that someone was burning a field in the spring and it got away from them and your place looks like the end of a cigar in a train station pisspot.

And then you'll hear that your lake is turning into Windex from acid rain, and pretty soon what you got is fifty acres of the moon. If the West Germans want fifty acres of the moon, they don't have to go to Nova Scotia to get it. They can buy a slag heap from a strip mine. What I'm saying is, right now, you got a piece of property that looks like a piece of the earth used to look before we fucked it up too much. And for that, I can get you ten-five.'

She sat back on the sofa and took out a bag of Bull Durham from the bib pocket of her overalls, and an envelope of papers, and rolled herself a cigarette, sprinkling in the grains like crushed chillies. When she lit it, they sputtered and sparked.

Jack moved restlessly across the room and settled beside Thérèse at the fireplace. She was surprised, and looked up at him as he sat on the hearth, moving a pile of books aside.

'You said I was going to be rich,' he said at last.

Amy looked at Max as if for translation.

'You said I was going to be very very wealthy.'

'Did I?'

'On the phone.'

'Oh.'

'That's why I came.'

'Oh. Not for the chicken and the booze, huh?' She picked a seed off her lower lip. 'I get it. I get it. You think I'm holding something out on you, don't you? You think this is some kind of scam. I get it. Smart boy. You know what you want.' She looked at Thérèse. 'He knows what he wants, sister.'

'He wants to be rich,' she said, looking up at him. From beneath his jaw, he looked vulnerable, as if this were an audition or an exam. 'It's just that the word means something to him.'

'Begging your pardon, begging your pardon. I know ten-five don't make you rich. I was speaking hypothetically, my son, of the future. And I know that in the future you are going to be. . . uh, that word. You want to know how I know? Your name.

You ever think about that? How your name sounds? Sure you have. You must have. Try it out: Jack Milford!'

She stretched a banner across the sky with her hand.

'Jack Milford! Boy tycoon! It works, eh? Some names work, some names don't. Take mine, for example. Amy Berry. What does that sound like to you?'

'An author,' Thérèse said impulsively.

'Yeah? Not bad, not bad. What of?'

'A . . . an exercise book!'

She laughed with a jingling sound, as if her lungs were full of keys. 'Yeah! *Amy Berry's No-Weight-Loss-Diet Book!* Well, you could be right, you could be right. One thing for sure, it ain't no rich name. No, kiddo, I ain't trying to con you. I just don't have the name for it.'

'May I speak?' Max said. 'I think there is something more than money bothering our young entrepreneur here this evening. Am I right?'

Jack let him continue.

'May I be so bold as to surmise that it has something to do with what I may or may not have said last meeting about the dubious moral fibre of certain of the neighbouring habituées? And, I gather that young Mr. Milford has not been remiss in his homework, but has found out something else about the Forrest property, something which leaves him somewhat iffy about unloading it into innocent hands, shall we say. Hmmm?'

'Huh?' Amy said.

'He has scruples, in other words.'

'Oh.'

'Let me take a guess. You think you have purchased the Amityville Horror.'

Amy cackled at that. 'Not a chance! I sold the Amityville Horror last month a professor from Dal. Handyman's Paradise. Good Starter Home. Rustic Charm.'

'Am I close?'

'Pretty close,' Jack said.

'Right, then.' Max popped lightly his lips on his pipe. 'Now we're getting somewhere. Nature of the complaint?'

'Unanswered questions.'

'Unanswered by whom?'

'By you.'

'By me! Ohhh!'

'But I haven't asked you yet.'

'I see. Most interesting. And you are going to.'

'Now.'

'I see. How delightful. I enjoy twenty questions.' He sucked on his pipe and a strand of twist hanging out of the bowl ignited and dropped a squirming orange cinder into his lap where it puffed out in a burning tweed smell, but he did not seem to notice. 'Ask away, then.'

'Who was crazy, the Goetz family or the Forrest family?'

'Neither. And both.'

'No games.'

'Indeed not. It is not a riddle. It is your answer.'

'Trouble with the word *crazy?*'

'A little. Let's say, damaged.'

'Brain damaged?'

'Good boy.'

'From what?'

'From birth.'

'Which family?'

'The only family.'

'No games!'

Thérèse looked up, and there was a beading of sweat on Jack's upper lip as if something inside him were cooking.

'I am not playing. I said the only family. The only one.'

'Which one.'

'The one.'

Max was smiling benignly, Amy too. They looked suddenly alike.

'The one family.'

'That's right.'

'There is only one family.'

'You are correct.'

Jack blinked his eyes squeezing the sweat out of them.

'Only one family because . . .'

'Because? Come on, you know why. From the first time you stepped foot into my surgery. That man ahead of you, the bleeding one. Come on! Think! Blood that loves to bleed.'

'Hemophilia,' Jack sighed.

'The Kings' Legacy. Because they kept the strain pure, the royal strain, the royal family line, unadulterated by outside influence.'

'Inbreeding.'

'Precisely.'

'Incest.'

'When and wherever possible.'

'The one family.'

'Only one.'

'How big?'

'How big do you want?'

'Two households? More? The whole community?'

'How big do you want?'

The doctor smiled around the room, and Amy Berry smiled with him.

'Where does it stop? Who is not affected by it? I am a doctor, and I don't know. I see them coming to me with babies who cannot hold their heads up in the cradle so they collapse their own windpipes with the weight of their dropsical heads. I see infants who have howled out their guts in ignorant agony with umbilical hernias like birthday balloons. I see them grow up slope-foreheaded so you almost expect their knuckles to drag in the dust. And then there are the other ones you wouldn't suspect. They get driver's licenses just like anybody else. They can buy and sell land. They are free men. With maybe no more trace than a tendency to bleed around the body orifices. A little extra leakage, that's all. And once in a great while I get someone who develops a swelling, fibrous, in the jaw or the forehead usually, not malignant, not painful, but unsightly, and I can remove it with a local anaesthetic. I do that, rather than refer them to the hospital. The hospital would not understand, but I'm used to it. I open up those swollen pouches of their skin, and out come little pieces of somebody else, bones of a foot unformed, like limp spaghetti *al dente,* like a bird embryo. Once I got what was going to be someone's ear. It looked like a little dried apricot. These little brothers and sisters of brothers and sisters inside each other, the body all mixed up at what's going on. Where does it stop, do you know?

'What do you want to do, send in a birth control squad like they ship over to Pakistan? It's too late, I tell you. You can lecture them, but the deed was done long ago. It started and it won't end, and as long as I'm doctor here, I'll keep snipping off the vestigial tails that grow in around eighteen months. They miss that at the hospital usually, nothing more than a pimple on the coccyx then, unless you know what you're looking for. They don't mind bringing them in when it's grown to be a caterpillar sac of flesh. I snip it off. Snip snip. No questions asked. Snip snip.'

He was stone cold sober.

'Snip snip.'

He made the motion with his fingers.

'Snip snip.'

Amy mimicked him.

'Snip snip. Over and done with. Don't give it a second thought. See you in another six weeks. Bye now.'

'My God!' Jack said. 'All of them? Everyone? It's spread everywhere? Even into the town?'

'How big do you want?'

The doctor opened his arms. Amy followed his gesture.

'How big do you want?'

'Is that why the place has no name? Does everyone know?'

'Of course it has a name. Every place has a name. Just because there is no highway sign and because it is not on the map doesn't mean it has no name. I'm sure it's a name you've heard before.'

'What is it?' He remembered Tres' question: *Where do we live?*

'The old people called it Sidon.'

'I've never heard of it.'

'Think for a minute.'

'Is it in the Mid-East?' Thérèse said.

'Good girl!'

'Was there some trouble there?'

'There certainly was. Back in the days of Ezekiel.'

'No, I mean just recently. Wasn't there a bombing or a high-jacking or something?'

'And I mean back in the days of Ezekiel. "For I will send into her pestilence, and blood into her streets." '

He blinked at the two of them as if a bright light had been shone on him.

'Blood into her streets.'

He blinked blindly at Amy. She came to stand beside him. She was small enough that her head came just above his shoulder where he was seated. She put both hands on his shoulder and blinked in the same way, something stunned by the light.

'Blood. Of kings.'

Max laid his head gently on Amy's hands, nestling his beard against her fingers.

'How can you stay?' Jack said.

Max lifted his head slowly to reply.

'Kings, Mr. Milford. The Kings and Queens of crested courts. Kings and Queens and Dukes and Earls, Viceroys and Dauphins and Dutchesses and Lords and Ladies. The Kings' Legacy, Squire Milford! Welcome to your new neighbours, and your new family!'

'But where are they? Why are they hiding?'

'They're waiting to see if you will go or stay. They are shy.

Even gentle, some of them. They are waiting to see if you will stay. Then they will come to see you. They know you are waiting for them. Your brothers and your sisters.'

THERESE HAD TO DRIVE HOME. HE COULD NOT CONTROL THE car. He flattened the accelerator pedal to the floor or let the car coast almost to a stop. She changed places with him in the middle of the dark road. He did not even pull the car to the shoulder. There were no other cars, no lights except their own. Yet, as she crossed through the bug-clustering beams of the headlights, she had a sense that there were dark houses near her on the road. It was a feeling such as she had experienced the first night, waking up parked by their house, as if she were inside a tunnel.

She found the turn to their drive with no trouble. It was becoming familiar.

THAT NIGHT, JACK DREAMT HE WAS IN A WOOD, AND THERE WAS knee-high growth that brushed his naked legs wetly as he tried to pass through. But it was not green growth, it was pale flesh growth, and it was seeding itself, flippers of flesh seeded with a dew of milky semen sown through the forest by a cock like an arm that scattered the seed in the spray of an arc, a fan to left and right and wherever the semen landed, something fleshy sprang up. The fleshy things slapped at his legs as he tried to pass through, brainless reaching things, eyeless touching things, still they were holding him back until he could not move for stepping on them. He knew if he did step on them, they would cry out with a horrible cry, and yet they were being seeded ever deeper by that sowing cock.

It was his own cock.

He had it in both his hands, and it was pumping his palms full and running between his fingers and onto the sheets.

He lay still to hear if he had wakened her. He held his breath.

X

It was hot already when Jack drove the Renault into Clifton Bridge, though the sun was still low and came in the windshield into his eyes. He dropped the visor and still had to steer with one hand slanted before his brow, until he turned to follow the river. In places, the river bottom was exposed, pebbly like the inside of a sock, as if turned inside out. An ache was growing above his right temple. It was a kernel now. He had wakened with it.

Thérèse had said she did not want to come with him. He had thought she would not want to stay at the house alone but she had wanted even less to come into town.

'I know what you'll do,' she said. 'You'll go into that store and you'll start buying more things to put in the house.'

He could not believe she was joking about it.

'Didn't you hear what the old goat was saying? Do you think I'm staying here?'

She was putting on a black Lycra swimsuit, one-piece, with a scooped back. The cool linoleum felt good under her bare feet.

'Doctors always sound scary like that,' she said. 'They know so many things the rest of us never see. It must make them a little crazy, I think.'

'So, it did frighten you, what he said.'

'No. Not frighten, really. I think, it made me sad, a little. Sad for those people.'

'You're not frightened to stay home alone?'

'Why would I be frightened?' she said, stripping the quilt off the bed to take outdoors. 'He said they were harmless. "Gentle," he said.'

She came with Jack out to the car. He stood by it with the sun glinting off the roof into his eyes. He could smell his shirt. It was a smell not of labour but of strain. A smell wrung out of him. He should have changed but he did not want to touch the suitcase until he packed it and they left. Together.

He was standing with the car door open as if he were the visitor, leaving.

'What are you going to do here while I'm gone?'

'I'm going to sunbathe, and if I feel like it, I may even do my floor exercises.'

'It's going to be hot.'

'I can go indoors if I like. There's lots of room inside. You know, I think you should keep it that way. Unfurnished. I like it. That big room, the parlour? It has a good floor for dancing. I want you to save that room for me. Don't bring back a lot of things, okay?'

'Don't you want to come in with me for breakfast?'

'No,' she said, tossing the roll of quilt over her shoulder, 'I do not want your breakfast. I do not want to go into town with you. I want to be alone here. I like being alone. You do not leave me enough alone.'

'You. . .like it here?'

She cocked her head and smirked at him. 'I hate it here. It is an awful place. But, you know what? One time I was a little girl and my mother took me to visit some people she knew who had a little cottage on one of the lakes, I think it was Lake Erie, and when we got there, we found that the lake was dead. On the beach there were dead fish washed up like sand. It was something the cities were putting in the water. There was a smell everywhere, a stink like bad cabbage. But, you know? There were people in the water. Little boys were playing in the water right at the edge, floating little boats they had made out of wood. They just kicked the dead fish away and walked through. There was a black dog going after a stick. There were people in canoes. At first I thought, how can these people do this without getting sick, without dying of it? But we stayed there the weekend, and the more I saw the people in the water, the more I thought, it doesn't kill them, it won't kill me, and I became less afraid of the dead lake. And I even got used to the smell. So I went in the water. And look. I didn't die.'

93

She shifted the weight of the quilt. She wanted him to hurry up and go.

'Jack, I can get used to anything. This is where I am now. I can lie down in the sun on a little blanket, and I don't care where I am. I could be on the rooftop in Montreal with tar and TV aerials all around me. Jack, it's the way I am. You don't know that. You still don't know that. I make myself happy. That's what I do. You want to be the provider, all right, you can think that you are the provider. But you don't provide for me. You see? I'm not eating. I don't care if the house is empty. I don't care if the grass isn't mowed. When I lay down my blanket, it flattens everything out, and when I lie down on top of it, that's where I am, just lying in the sun. I don't think "Who owns this? Is this mine?" If someone wants to come along and tell me "Get off, this isn't your place," all right, I'll go. I'll find someplace else.'

'I'm selling it,' Jack said.

'Good,' said Thérèse, going between the scrawny apple trees to the backyard. 'I hope it makes you very happy.'

He could smell himself in the car, stronger as he got closer to town. He had not even tucked in his shirt. He would have to do something to make himself look better. Maybe he should stop first and buy a shirt. But new shirts always had creases in the wrong places, threads that were loose, and they itched. They needed to be washed first. He wondered if you could buy pre-washed shirts.

Maybe the smell wasn't so bad. Maybe Mrs. Berry wouldn't mind. Her office was small, and it would be cooking in the sun through the plate glass window on Queen Street, but the transaction would be quick; maybe she wouldn't notice.

He knew what the smell was now, being twisted out of him like wringing a towel. It was the smell of making money.

THE SUN ON THE EAST SIDE OF THE HOUSE WAS TOO HOT. Thérèse lay in it on the quilt as long as she could stand. There were still low clouds of morning fog sheeting overhead, and when the sun broke through it made the rusted tin roof on the barn tick with tortured expansion, and Thérèse felt it clamp over her exposed skin. Then like the last of a bridal train, the overcast was gone and she was held down under the heat, as if under glass. She lay on her stomach, her head turned to one side, then the other, eyes squeezing shut against the glare, and she smelled the old quilt baking. It smelled like bread, and with her eyes closed, in the stupor of the heat, she imagined that bread dough and cotton stuffing were the same thing, that the world had produced a food you could sleep in. It was the kind of thought she had, like a dream, that seemed so true until she opened her eyes.

She felt the hair on the back of her head and was alarmed. It was burning up! Too hot to touch!

She drew her knees under her and crouched a moment before sitting up. She knew she would be dizzy. When she raised her head and looked around her, the world seemed newly painted in the sunshine. Her eyes spun around the vista of the waving heads of timothy just off the lawn and the old maple with its stocky trunk and the lower limbs parallel with the ground reaching out like the beams of a house. The narrow neck of the lake was pocked by a little breeze she could not feel up by the house so that the water seemed to be dimpled by a myriad of insects. Still on her hands and knees she turned on the quilt and she could see the far shore where the baptism had been, could make out the two boulders, like little pastel eggs now, and then the lower end of the lake where there was a reflection now of the trees, imperfect, as if in wavy glass of an old window, and then the nearer trees and the barn and carriage shed, their roofs seeming burnished by the sun, and then the grey wall of her own house that seemed to lie on its side, its knees drawn up in the ell, sheltering her.

Her gaze had spiraled like the grooves on a record, and come back to her at the centre, like a magical record she had imagined as a child, that would play something different every time you put down the needle, because you would never set the needle down in exactly the same place, and where you started it determined what it would play. A record with only one side and infinite variations. A record that never ended because the last groove took it back to the beginning again with a loop like a spider's trail.

And her gaze had told her something else. She was alone.

THE KERNEL HAD BECOME A NUT, A FILBERT KNOTTED UNDER THE skin. Jack worked at it with the fingers of his right hand as he looked in through the glass at the empty office of Dominion Realtors. He did not know why she did not call it Berry Realty. She was obviously the only person who worked here, and even she never seemed to work here. It must be something like what she said about a name. It had certainly fooled him. When he had seen the little box ad in the back pages of the *Gazette* offering lake frontage, isolated retreats, island homes, he had thought of Dominion Realtors as a broad chain. Standing here at the empty office, he felt like a fevered, bitten discoverer who stands at the headwater spring of a great river, and sees that it is a pissy trickle and has nowhere else to go.

He went to The Smoke Shoppe. There was one other man at the counter. He had his mug. It said in exultant, perking brown letters HOT MUGGA! All the other mugs were in their places on the wall including Mrs. Berry's.

'Is it customary to leave the office open when nobody's in it?' Jack said, looking distastefully into his cup. There was a pearl of styrofoam floating in the black.

'Mondays are slow,' the girl said.

'You might find her down at the post office,' said the man, getting up to go, giving his mug back to the girl. She rinsed it out in the sink under the counter, and hung it back in its place, completing the set.

'You're not from around here,' the man said, as if he were telling Jack something new.

'I just bought. . . some property.'

He had thought of naming it. Why hadn't he? Afraid that the man hadn't heard the name Forrest? Or afraid that he had?

'Summer place, is it?'

'Could be. I'm thinking of. . . I'm going to sell it.'

'What's the matter?' said the man, grinning. 'Don't you like it around here?'

HOT MUGGA.

It was a good name for him. He stood in the door, not waiting for Jack to reply, but thinking about what would be his parting word.

'You want to be here in the fall. Summer time is for suckers. Now me, I got a nice piece of real estate right by the ocean. I don't live there, mind you. I got a little summer cottage the wife and I fixed up. I might go down there for overnight. Sunday barbecue. That kind of thing. But the summer people! They stop right on the highway and try to buy the place off me. See me sitting in the shade and they think I want to sell. They just look at it and they want it. They think it's that easy. They'll buy anything in the summer. They'd buy my old fish shack if it was for sale. They just see it like it's a painting on a wall and they want it. "It must be marvelous being able to come down any time you want," they say. They're just on a two or three week vacation, see. Got to make the best of it. It must be marvelous living here. I tell them, "Once or twice a year you think you're in heaven, the rest of the time you could slit your throat." They don't believe me.'

Hot Mugga went out the door.

'Will there be anything else?' the girl said.

He had not touched his coffee. He did not want to have to talk to the girl. If he waited at the counter, he would be able to watch the street and see Mrs. Berry come back to the office but it was not the only place he could wait. He had thought of someone else on the town he could visit, someone he had almost forgotten he knew, like forgetting whether someone famous is alive or dead. But this person, he at least knew, was alive.

'Can I use your phone?'

'There was no pay phone, but she showed him where the phone was in the back room, beside a stack of cartons of ice cream cones. *Cornettes* they were called in translation.

'If it's a local number, you can just dial 3.'

'I don't know the number.'

'I think there's a book around here somewhere.'

'It's a new listing.'

'Oh. I don't know what you do then.'

He dialed 'O.'

THE ROOM WAS PERFECT FOR DANCING. IT WAS NOT LONG, BUT IT was big enough for her alone, and high, and almost square, taking up all of the ell except for the little birthing room. But the best thing about it was that it was empty.

She began by stretching and loosening. She could do this anywhere, she did not need much room, but she liked standing in the centre, feeling that she could stretch and stretch and never reach the wall or ceiling. The floor was surprisingly clean for an old house. She checked it with her hand before she sat down to work on the lower back and the thighs and the feet. Of course her feet would be black when she finished. They always were, no matter how clean the floor. But she did not want to bring in the old quilt, the oilcloth felt so cool on the backs of her legs. It had been printed to look like a rug, with a border and even the image of fringe. It showed the ridges of the boards underneath, but it had not cracked yet. She pulled herself up out of her spine, as she had been taught, and pointed and flexed her feet, so that her calves came off the floor. That was another thing about a hard floor. It did not give, so you knew just how much work you were doing.

When she had finished the floor exercises, she went to the west window which faced up the hill. The sill was too low, really, to use as a *barre*, but it was wide and sturdy. She put her heel up on it anyway, and when she bent close to her knee, her face to the side, she could see herself in the windowglass, almost like a mirror. She reversed and worked on the other side. From here she could see the shadow thrown by the house on the front lawn. It looked like a tall, cool mountain.

She faced the *barre* squarely with both hands on it, fingers as light as if on a keyboard, and did her *pliés,* and on the first one there was a satisfying pop in her lower back and she thought, 'Good,' and used the muscles to tuck her back in more until she could take her hands off the *barre* entirely, her back straight as a wall, bending low and rising tall, making the view out the window sink and swell like the view out a porthole of a ship at sea, and she released one arm slowly, curved like a seagull's wing to sweep in and out to her rising and falling, and she looked serenely, blissfully at the arc of the arm ending in the slightest gesture of invitation in the curl of the fingers. It was what called her partner to her side.

She was ready. She took her place in the centre of the room. Pity there was no music.

She would make the rhythm with her feet and her breathing. Something fast.

OF COURSE THE OLD MAN WOULD HAVE A PHONE. HE HAD HAD one in the old house, he would have one in his new apartment. Old people wanted a phone handy, so they could call for a prescription, for a delivery, for an ambulance.

He got the address from Directory Assistance. The operator was in Halifax. They weren't supposed to give out addresses, didn't he know that? He got it out of her easily.

'I'm not sure of the first name.'

'I have a Forrest, E.'

'Gee, I don't remember. Is it a Prince Street address?'

'I have a Forrest, E. on Pleasant Street.'

'Thank you.'

He did not call. Somehow he thought that if he called to say he was coming, by the time he hung up and got there, the man would be gone. And it was easy enough to find the new apartment building on Pleasant Street.

Jack felt a kind of pride as he looked through the index of names by the buttons in the lobby of the building. The lobby was a concrete and plaster entry, between two glass doors, neither of them locked, with decorative swirls of the trowel in the ceiling, and a wrought iron arabesque holding a tavern light with amber plastic for glass.

My thirty-five hundred, he thought.

The old man was in, of course. Doing nothing. Sitting at his chrome set in the narrow kitchen with a cup of tea. It was a dainty cup and saucer with pictures in a crest commemorating a visit of the King and Queen to Canada, and it was bad tea, dark as radiator fluid. The old man pretended to be pleased, but he was suspicious. He acted as if he thought Jack had come to sell something. He reminded Jack of the young man and woman who had come to their door in Montreal, looking like people whose names you have forgotten, and they said, 'Are you a young couple?' and laughed, and Jack said, 'You're not selling encyclopedias, are you?' and laughed, and expected them to tell him they had just moved in and were looking for some company, someone to finish a bottle of wine with, directions to a good cheap restaurant, advice on how to make the rear burner on the stove work, and slowly the uneasiness went away as they asked about him and his wife and his job and her career and he invited them in and they sat side by side and complimented the room, and then it turned out that, yes, they were selling encyclopedias.

Mr. Forrest gave Jack the one cup of tea and no more. He waited apprehensively for the reason for his coming, but he wasn't afraid Jack was going to sell him something. He was afraid he was going to take something away.

'You ain't here to get your money back, is you?' he said at last, trying for a laugh that came out as a hiss between his teeth.

'Why would that be?'

'Oh, I thought the damn Sidonites drove you out.'

'Sidonites?'

'It's what we call 'em. You must have seen 'em. Don't tell me Pastor Loomer ain't been down to try to sell you their damn foolishness.'

'What, you mean his church?'

'Church? It ain't no church. You see a church anywheres around?'

'Well, no, but I thought...'

'Mister man, that bunch you keep well away from. You married? Children? Any girls? If it was me, living there still, and I had any girls, I'd see to it that that bunch was locked up.'

'What do you mean? It's not against the law to be a Baptist in Nova Scotia is it?'

'Baptist!' His laughter sprayed the table cloth. 'They ain't Baptists! *I'm* a Baptist, if you want to know. They're Sidonites, is what they are.'

'You mean from the old name?'

'That's right. Nobody uses that name anymore. Best off forgotten. Who'd want to go around naming a place Sidon? Would you, knowing what it says in the Bible? You do read your Bible, don't you? You heard of Sidon?'

'Yes, I...'

'It'd be like naming the place Sodom or Gomorrah. Who'd want to do that? Crazy old people.'

He didn't mean old people, he meant the people of old, but saying it made him seem suddenly not old himself, as if escaping from the house and land and getting through the magic glass doors had saved him from aging, as if Apartment 6 on the ground floor with the avocado tinted stove and fridge was Shangri La.

'You seen any of their women? You see what they do to them? End up lookin like somethin in a sack. Even somethin in a sack'd look better than that. Better if you couldn't see it at all. No colour. No shape. You see the men? They got about as much life in 'em as a popple tree. That's what they do, take the life right out of you. Turn you to wood. That's a Sidonite for you. They go right down to the last thing, the one thing a man and a woman was put on the earth to do, and they take the fun right out of it. You know what I'm talkin about, don't you?'

Jack felt queasy. He did not want to hear the old man talk about this.

'There's lots of other gospel churches and all tell you about fornication, make you scared of it, and there's some of 'em even tries to make you not want to do it. But they can't do that, eh? Sidonites got that figured out. They ain't gonna keep their men off their women, they know that. It'll just send 'em elsewhere, or out to the barn. And they can't let 'em breed like rabbits. Not that they wouldn't mind havin their congregation grow. But just that it would be too much fun. So they got to take the fun out of it. How? They tell their men, all right, you can stick your pecker in there, you can move it around and push and shove on it all you want, anytime you want, but the one thing you ain't allowed to do is finish it off. You know what I'm talkin about? I ain't talkin about spillin your seed on the ground like Onan. I'm talking about not spillin your seed at all!'

'You mean . . . ?'

'That's what they tell their men, damn Loomer and his bunch. You can do it by the power of the mind, they say. Power of the mind. You can stop your seed by the power of the mind. You know what that's going to do to a man when he gets inside a woman and he's allowed to make it feel as good as he wants, but he knows he can't finish it off? Know what that's bound to do? That's bound to drive a man crazy, that is. That's power of the mind for you.'

THE DANCE FILLED THE ROOM. USE THE SPACE, SHE HEARD HER instructor telling her. I want you to use all of the space! Feel the space! Touch the space! Make it work for you!

She stirred the room into a frenzy. The rhythm of her heels and the slap of the flat of her foot as she leaped through space and the woodsawing sound of her breath were joined now by her heartbeat, stepping up the tempo. She was like a bee in a jar shaken to madden it, but now she was shaking the space, and when she landed once she felt her teeth click. She knew she was too tense, but it was a dance to build the room, to build it the way she wanted to, it was a dance of hammer and nails, spiking the space into what she wanted, and she didn't care if it was good or not. This was what she got without music. Okay. This was her dance for today, and it was the way she was feeling today.

Her wrists snapped and her arms cut the air, cutting back, keeping away, slicing down, her hand a blade, back, *Back!* She spun, the balls of her feet shrieking with each twist, black she knew, no resin for them, they would bleed afterwards, it was not the first time, it was all right, it was what happened. She spun on the diagonal across the room, her arms whipping her faster, her feet ripping into whorls on the floor now spattered with her sweat, like a drill gone mad and skittering out of control, but she was in control, she was gravity, the centripetal force, the impetus the spindle of all centres the driveshaft the axle of what she was, and she could make herself stop, and she did make herself stop, just where she wanted, right on the mark, absolute zero, the frozen arrest of all motion, in the corner of the room by the wall with the window.

She held for the release, as if waiting for the applause.

She was not being applauded.

But she was being watched.

JACK COULD NOT MAKE THE OPERATOR UNDERSTAND. THERE WAS a knot like the swollen bole on a tree inside his head, and he had to hold the receiver away from his ear but it didn't matter if he could hear her or not, she would not understand.

'But I received a call myself at that number just last night! Ring 24! Two long and four short rings! Why can't you understand that?'

'What name did you say?'

'It's not in anyone's name! I thought the phone was disconnected, it used to be in the name of . . . oh, never mind, but I just moved in and I haven't had the phone put in my name, I didn't think it was working, but it rang! It rang two long and four short! Why can't you just ring the number for me?'

'I'm sorry, sir, but that number is disconnected.'

'I know it's disconnected! I already told you that! Just make it ring, damn you! My wife is home alone. She'll answer it. You'll see.'

'I'm sorry, sir, but . . .'

'Look, I don't know how she did it, but the central operator made it ring somehow. Just tell her to do it again.'

'I'm sorry, but central reports that number is disconnected.'

'It's an old phone, it's a hand crank, I don't know how you do it, make her push the button or whatever she does to make it ring. It hasn't been disconnected! I know!'

'I'm sorry, sir. If you wish to have the number re-installed, you will have to contact our service office.'

'Give me Clifton Bridge Central, Ring 24, goddamnit!'

She had not cut him off, but she had done whatever they were trained to do with a madman on the line. He heard the electric silence.

'It's outside of town. Out in the country. It's a little place. It's called Sidon.'

He thought he heard a breath. He thought he heard her lips open.

'There is no exchange by that name.'

XI

THE LITTLE RENAULT RACED AS IF ITS THROTTLE WERE STUCK.
Jack was grinding the pedal into the floor. He twisted the wheel
in both hands as if he would rip it off its stem, and when he
passed cars on the river road, he blew the horn like unfurling a
serpentine. He wanted them to hear the sound of emergency,
the Doppler siren of crisis. And he wanted to hurt the car. He
saw a red dashboard light flash out of the corner of his eye and
he didn't slacken one bit. Goddamn little cars! He had told
Thérèse, 'What do you want a big car for, all that power?
When are you going to use it? Passing? Going uphills?'

Rescuing your wife?

He saw his wife in a house surrounded by people, a crowd of
people keeping her in there by their ring of complicity, and
they watched her inside running from window to window as if
the house were on fire and she could not escape. The people
were in a carnival spirit. This was sport to them. It was like the
horrifying custom of the Shivaree he had seen in a movie about
the Irish. They were tromping on the roof to scare her,
throwing things against the glass, banging pots and pans, and
barking and yodeling like aboriginees flushing game.

Then he saw one of the men, the tallest one, with shirt
buttons straining and sleeves rolled up, urged into the house.
He had a jaw like a fire hydrant. He was tracking Tres through
the resounding halls, and he knew where to corner her. In the
birthing room. The birthing room. It was also the dying
room. When you were birthing or when you were dying, you
didn't want to go upstairs. And he nailed her against a wall.
Planked her, like planked salmon, pressed her and held her
with no hands, and then he did a thing you wouldn't think a
man would do. He took his one fist and drove it through the
plaster wall, made a hole like a fist in ice, through the lime dust
and the horsehair, and he pulled out a length of barbed wire. It
was what he used to tie her wrists. Her crown of thorns.

Though he didn't have to. She would have let him do it, easy. She was guiding him down on the floor, saying, 'Okay, it's all right, not so fast, not so fast, just let me . . .' and she was showing him how. And all around the house were faces pressed to the windows.

And later she could say, 'You don't have to be raped. You can let him do it. Then he won't hurt you. Most of them are impotent anyway. They don't know if they're in you or out of you. You can take them between your thigh muscles and they never know the difference. The thing is not to let them beat you. You don't want to get hurt. You didn't want me to get hurt, did you?'

Fucking bitch!

The worst of it was that it was happening without him. You can't be two places at the same time. You can't have everything. Goddamn the laws of nature!

Come on! Come on! he exhorted the car. But it had no more to give, and the needle stayed at a hundred.

THERESE BACKED AWAY FROM THE WINDOW. SHE DID NOT WANT to see what it was. It was still there, she was sure, it had not moved, but she did not want to see. She moved out of sight, backing toward the birthing room door, and suddenly she felt, in the black bathing suit in the barren room, like a tryout for a blue movie on videotape. She saw her gestures, a melodramatic hand to her mouth, arm upraised, tender wrist exposed, as if from above, as if the room had no ceiling, like a TV soundstage. She had always wondered who the women were. Now she thought that maybe they were women who had gone through something like this, and had acted it out later to exorcise their demons, being paid for it at the same time. Prisoner of Vikings. Lassie Goes Down. Randy Sailors in Town. Three Big Cum Scenes. Gang Bang. Ape Rape. Splash!

All she had to do to get out of the movie was to walk back to the window and see who it was. But it was like violating the script, forgetting to count. It was like walking offstage in audition. It was something she had never done. And then she thought, Improvise! The last thing the director would expect. It was like taking the chance of being laughed at, or hired.

She walked back to the window. A stagey walk, but it got her there. Face to face.

WHEN THE CAR WOULD NOT HOLD THE ROAD ON THE CORNERS, IT bit into the dirt shoulder, with a sound like a lathe tearing at the rubber. He passed the doctor's house with the driveway full of cars. It looked like a party. He sailed over a rise by a highway sign that said Blind Crest with a picture of a toy car on an inclined plane, and his head pressed against the padded ceiling of the compartment and he landed half out of the bucket seat. He was daring the domain of physics. You can't make time stand still. You can't turn the clock backward. He did not think about the law, or innocent pedestrians. He thought about being the first man in space. It wasn't Houston Control and digital readouts. It was this. Hanging on.

SHE LOOKED INTO THE EYES. JUST BY STAYING THERE, SHE WAS giving an invitation. The face drifted past the window, like a helium balloon at the end of the day.

She heard the screen door open.

HE WAS LOOKING FOR LANDMARKS, LIKE CONSTELLATIONS. IN A moment of panic, he thought he had missed the turn, he was driving past their road. He would skim off the end of the mainland and skip across the water, someone's wish. There were no houses, all the turns looked the same. Old Forrest was right, there was no church. He had thought it was up a side road somewhere, but the man was right. They met in the Loomers' house. Where was the road to their house? He didn't know. It would be right before his own driveway, but he had never found it. Or maybe it didn't cut straight to the highway, maybe it curved around and around somewhere. How would he know if he had gone too far, then, thinking about astronauts? He would have to wait and see. You'll have to wait and see. You'll know it when you get there. If you have to ask, don't ask.

Now!

Left!

He powered down the hill into the green tunnel, and something in the underbody of the car was left behind on the hump of the drive with a ping of compliant metal.

He could see the house.

It was not surrounded by people. There was no one there. That was just as bad.

Then he saw a figure pass the window in the ell, and it was not his wife, he knew that.

He aimed for the window, and just before the car hit, he thought, I could kill myself so he let go of the wheel and lay down sideways across both front seats, slipping out of the shoulder strap and secured by only the lap belt. It was what he had been told you should do, by the first man he admired, a boy really, his own age, in high school. The boy made money totalling cars for the insurance, and he told Jack how he did it. Jack could not bring himself to do it then, but he admired the boy nonetheless. That was what flashed before your eyes. Not your whole life. Just somebody you admired, maybe saving your life.

It worked.

The Renault hit the side of the house, launched slightly by the upgrade of the lawn, smack beside the parlour window, shattered the panes and the sash, and leaving a hole, as if workmen needed it to get their wheelbarrows through.

The car settled upright, and its hood, as if in afterthought, sprang open. There was no steam, no fire, and Jack was able to unbuckle himself and get out. There were a few shingles off the west wall. And he assumed the front end of the car was a mess, headlights and grill. Expensive things, he was thinking.

Then he looked at the hole in the wall where the window had been. It looked like an order window for a beach canteen now. Thérèse came to look out at him.

'Now look what you've done,' she said.

He knew what he'd done.

'You've scared her away.'

He did not know who *her* was.

XII

THEY DID NOT SPEAK UNTIL AFTER CROSSING THE MARSHES AT Amherst, except to say, 'Excuse me, I'm sorry I didn't see you, That's okay I've got it, Don't bother.' When Jack stopped at the Irving station to have new headlamps put in, Thérèse sat in the car and wouldn't speak. She sat in the car, too, when he parked briefly in front of Dominion Realtors on Queen Street. She didn't ask him when he came out if everything had gone all right — if he had explained about the broken window, if the carton of kitchenware made up for the cost, if he carried the certified cheque in his wallet or his shirt pocket. She looked at her reflection in the plate glass and she knew she was seeing a woman who was never coming back.

It was the ominous silence and the monotony of the New Brunswick pulpland that made her speak at last.

'I wanted to take her with me, you know, and you scared her away. I almost had her trusting me. She was like a little scared rabbit. And then you did...*that.*'

He nodded, speechless. It was his penitence. That, and driving.

'You didn't see her. She was like something that stands up out of the grass when you frighten it. She was just watching me dance. She didn't think I would see her but when I did, she froze. Like when you hit them with your headlights in the night, and their eyes are like marbles. You wonder what they are thinking of, why they don't get out of the way. Her mind was like that. She was just waiting to see if I would run over her or what, and then because I was quiet and calm and didn't say a word, and because I was a woman, too, I think, she knew I wouldn't hurt her, and she came indoors. She was the beginning of something, Jack, and you tried to run her down!'

He started to protest, but caught himself. He would drive until dark and let her talk. He would drive until they got to Québec, until they ran out of gas...

'She looked like him, you know. She had that same kind of nose, like a little boiled potato, but she had someone's long silken hair, black. Her mother's, I suppose. I think it's their religion that makes her keep it long, but I told her it was beautiful. I think that was the first time anyone had told her that. Certainly not boys at school. They would have thought only about the funny nose and the long dresses she had to wear. I think she's not allowed to think that she's beautiful, but it seemed all right for me to say it, and it got her talking.

' "You're a dancer," she told me. "We're not allowed to dance. Dancing is Satan inside you."

' "Do I look like I've got Satan inside me?" I said.

' "Maybe for you, dancing is a way of getting Satan out."

'I let her touch my bathing suit. My "costume," she called it. She was wearing this long dress, on that hot hot day, too, and high, thick white stockings, and lace-up boy's shoes. I let her touch the fabric, and she wanted to touch my arms, and I let her. She said, "You're so skinny!" and she asked me was it hard staying so thin, and I said the one thing I dreamed about sometimes, the one thing that would almost make me give up dancing, was pizza. And she said, "What does it taste like?"

'How do you explain what pizza tastes like to a seventeen-year-old girl? Today! When there are men on the moon and shuttle rocket ships, and a girl has never tasted pizza!

'I wanted to take her with us. I thought of it in about half a minute. I would talk her father into it. We would stay for the summer and I would be trying to talk him into it all the time, and when it was time for her to go off to Bible College, instead she would come stay with us in Montreal. Like an *au pair*.

'She was so sad! I think she had come down over the hill just walking, to get away. I don't think she meant to spy on us, though maybe her father told them about us. Maybe he *warned* them about us, and that was why she came down. Jack, she was the one girl who should not have stayed in that family. I know I've never met the rest of them and I've never seen their house, but she should have been given the chance. You know her married sister? The marriage was arranged. She hadn't even met the boy until she was nineteen and it was time for her to get married. He's a teacher at a Christian School, whatever that is. You could see the girl—Jack, damn you, you didn't even let me find out her name! She never even told me her name! —you could see she was different.

'You know what she told me? She told me in the fall, her father makes them rake the leaves in front of the house, all right, but he makes them rake the leaves *out* of the trees too! As high up as they can reach with a rake, they have to shake them out, because it saves time that way. And because the colour is sinful, too, I guess. Or it's sinful thinking it's beautiful. Or I don't know. Jack, it's so sad.'

He drove along the St. John River in the twilight. He didn't know where he was going to stop, but he drove and he let Tres cry. She rested her cheek on a fist and kept her face turned away from him, and her window was down partway to let in the air, and the sound of the wind covered her crying, but he knew he should let her. She had talked herself into it. It *was* sad. Even the telling of it was sad.

Finally she straightened with a shuddery breath and said simply, 'I hate them.'

'They're not. . .' Jack began.

'No. I hate them. I hate them all. I don't hate her, but I hate all the rest of them.'

He spoke softly, to see if she would let him.

'They're not to blame.'

'Hmm?' she said, as if she had not heard him.

'Don't blame them.'

'I do.'

'You can't, Tres. They haven't done anything.'

'What do you mean they haven't done anything? Don't you hear me telling you what that Loomer man is doing to his daughters, keeping them safe! Don't you remember what that fat *Anglais* told us? It was enough to make me sick! The house full of blood across the lake, the witch house. For God's sake, Jack, burning a chicken alive and pouring piss down your chimney! "How big do you want," he kept saying. "How big do you want." '

'Tres, it's none of it true!'

An oncoming car flashed its lights, and Jack turned his on.

'Oh, sure, I guess there were murders and things like that. Tres, don't tell me there aren't murders in Montreal! Right on our own block, Tres. What about the little girl they found tied up inside the super's flat in the building right next door, the one that had been missing for so long they thought she was dead, and he was feeding her out of a cat dish! Sure, that goes on here as well as elsewhere. But it never happened the way they said it happened. Don't you see? They all had their own side of the story. It doesn't mean one is lying and one is telling the truth. It just means they like to talk. People like to talk. And they like to talk about other people. You know what they say, "People will talk." That's what they do.'

'You mean, none of that . . .'

'It was just talk, Tres. And we were newcomers who hadn't heard it before.'

'But why? It was so horrible.'

'You can't blame them, Tres. You can hate them if you want to, but you can't blame them. They were just lonely.'

'Lonely! That's no way to get company, to tell stories about other people like that.'

'Maybe so. But what's the alternative? Wait for the world to come knocking at your door? You saw the house, you saw the roadside. We were there three days, and one person came knocking at our door.'

'One and a half.'

'Hell, in the suburbs they have frigging Welcome Wagons that come knocking on your door. But in the country...it's lonely, Tres. That's all. They didn't want to be left alone. Because that was the scariest of things. Not witchcraft and deformed babies and monsters coming out of your skin. Scarier than that is Nothing. No witches. No monsters. Just Nothing.

'You remember that movie we saw about the UFO's? Remember the movie poster? It looked real scary, with the UFO coming out of the night sky, and it had real scary letters that said, "WE ARE NOT ALONE."

'That was supposed to be scary, right? You know what it should have said? "WE SHOULD BE SO LUCKY."

'It's not scary thinking there's something out there. It's scary thinking there's nothing out there.

'Hell isn't other people, Tres. Hell is *no* other people.'

By the submarine light of the dashboard he saw her hands folded, palm up, in her lap. It was a position of calm for her, a yogic *mudra* of listening.

'Mr. Forrest had his side of the story, too, and it was just like everybody else's, but different. He hated to see me go when I left. I didn't even think of it at the time, I was so damn mad at that telephone and the people and...'

'...me.'

'...Yes...'

'For staying home.'

'Yes.'

'For staying home alone.'

'He was crying when I ran out, Tres. I didn't even think of it, I just thought he was an old man, old men cry, but he was trying to tell me about the auction. He said, "No one ever came to my house until I was selling out, and then they all came, but I might as well have been dead." '

'You were mad at me because I was alone.'

'Yes, I guess I was.'

'Why?'

'I . . . don't know, Tres. I just was.'

'Yes, you do know why, Jack Milford. You just said it. But you weren't talking about the other people, you weren't talking about movie posters. You were talking about yourself. You. You hate to be alone. You did know what you were doing to that old man there in that apartment where nobody comes because nobody ever came. And you were mad at me because I didn't seem to mind. And you couldn't stand me being alone and not minding it. But don't you see, Jack, it doesn't mean I want you to be alone. It doesn't mean I want to leave you. I don't want to leave you, Jack.'

The headlights of the traffic on the No. 2 turned into Christmas stars before his eyes.

'I don't want you to go, Tres.'

She put a hand on top of his hand on the wheel. 'Jack, I'll come back. I'll go away, but I'll come back.'

He squeezed his eyes, and the lights through his lashes radiated spokes of crystals like passing meteor brilliance.

'I'm going to miss you, Tres.'

She wiped his cheek with the back of a knuckle.

'I'm going to come back.'

THEY SHARED THE DRIVING, AND THAT WAY THEY CAME HOME with the dawn.

Readers, Take Advantage
of this Special Deal
on Three-Day Novels!

**THREE 3-DAY NOVELS
IN ONE:** Three winners of the
3-Day Novel Contest in one
package. Includes: *Still,
Accordion Lessons* by Ray
Serwylo, and *Dr. Tin* by Tom
Walmsley. A perfect gift for
your writer friends.
Three-In-One. $10.99

Single copies of the 3-Day Novels are also available:

Doctor Tin, by Tom Walmsley, is a contemporary *Pilgrim's
Progress*, following its alienated hero through three phases of his
violent, lascivious journey to heaven (or hell). Winner of the
1979 Contest. $4.95.

Accordion Lessons, by Ray Serwylo, is set in the Ukrainian
community of Winnipeg. A novel of cultural and personal self-
discovery. Winner of the 1981 Contest. $4.95

Still, by bp nichol. A first novel by the Governor-General's Award-
winning poet and well-known performer. $4.95

Order the Three-In-One Pack at $10.99, or single copies to suit
your taste. If your bookstore hasn't got them, use the coupon
overleaf for prompt delivery.

3-Day Novel Special Order Form

This is a direct purchase order—fill it in and mail it today. Your order will be filled within 72 hours of receipt. Cheques or money orders only. Please include the postal code with your address.

Please send me:

QUANTITY	PRICE	TOTAL
_____copies of **Three 3-Day Novels-In-One**	$10.99	_____
_____copies of **Still**	$ 4.95	_____
_____copies of **Accordion Lessons**	$ 4.95	_____
_____copies of **Doctor Tin**	$ 4.95	_____
Postage—please add 35¢ per item:		_____

TOTAL ENCLOSED: _____

Name: _____

Address: _____

_____

_____

Return to:
Pulp Press Book Publishers
986 Homer Street, No. 202
Vancouver, BC, Canada v6b 2w7

Jeff Doran is a writer who lives and works in rural Nova Scotia. His stories have been published in a number of magazines, including *Atlantic*, *Redbook* and *Saturday Night*. He claims W.O. Mitchell and William Faulkner as his major literary influences. As for the three days it took him to write *This Guest of Summer*, Doran says, "It was the greatest almost spiritual experience of my life."

A Note on the 3-Day Novel-Writing Contest

The Pulp Press International 3-Day Novel-Writing Contest began as a joke, became a dare, and is now in its way to becoming a literary institution. It has spawned what is probably the only genuinely Canadian genre in world literary history. The contest has been called a fad, an idle threat, a "great way to overcome writer's block," a "trial by deadline." It continues to fly in the face of the notion that novels take eight years of angst to produce and lush cash prizes to stimulate.

While a three-day contest is not in the business of producing deathless literature, we, as contest sponsors, continue to be amazed at the quality, depth and completeness of the entries we receive. Each year hundreds of writers bite the bullet and face the keys (or the pen or the video screen) over the Labour Day weekend, and submit their entries to the nearest participating sponsor. Sponsors are located at selected bookstores across the country.

Since its genesis in a Vancouver bar in 1978, the competition has generated hundreds of novels in several countries, made famous writers of such worthies as Tom Walmsley (1979 winner, for *Dr. Tin*) and Ray Serwylo (1981 winner, for *Accordion Lessons*), and an even more famous writer out of bpNichol, who was already fairly famous when he won the 1982 contest with *Still*. We're confident that future contests will discover other fine talents waiting for a suitable challenge.

First prize is a publishing offer from Pulp Press.

Contestants may register by phone, mail, or in person at their nearest sponsoring bookstore.

For more information, contact:
Pulp Press Book Publishers
986 Homer St., No. 202
Vancouver, B.C., Canada v6B 2w7
PH: (604) 687-4233